THE BAD SIDE OF GOOD

JASON CHANCE BOOK 4

JOSH GRIFFITH

Copyright © 2018 by Josh Griffith

All rights reserved.

No part of this book may be reproduced in any form or by any electronic or mechanical means, including information storage and retrieval systems, without written permission from the author, except for the use of brief quotations in a book review.

❀ Created with Vellum

For Francis Coppola

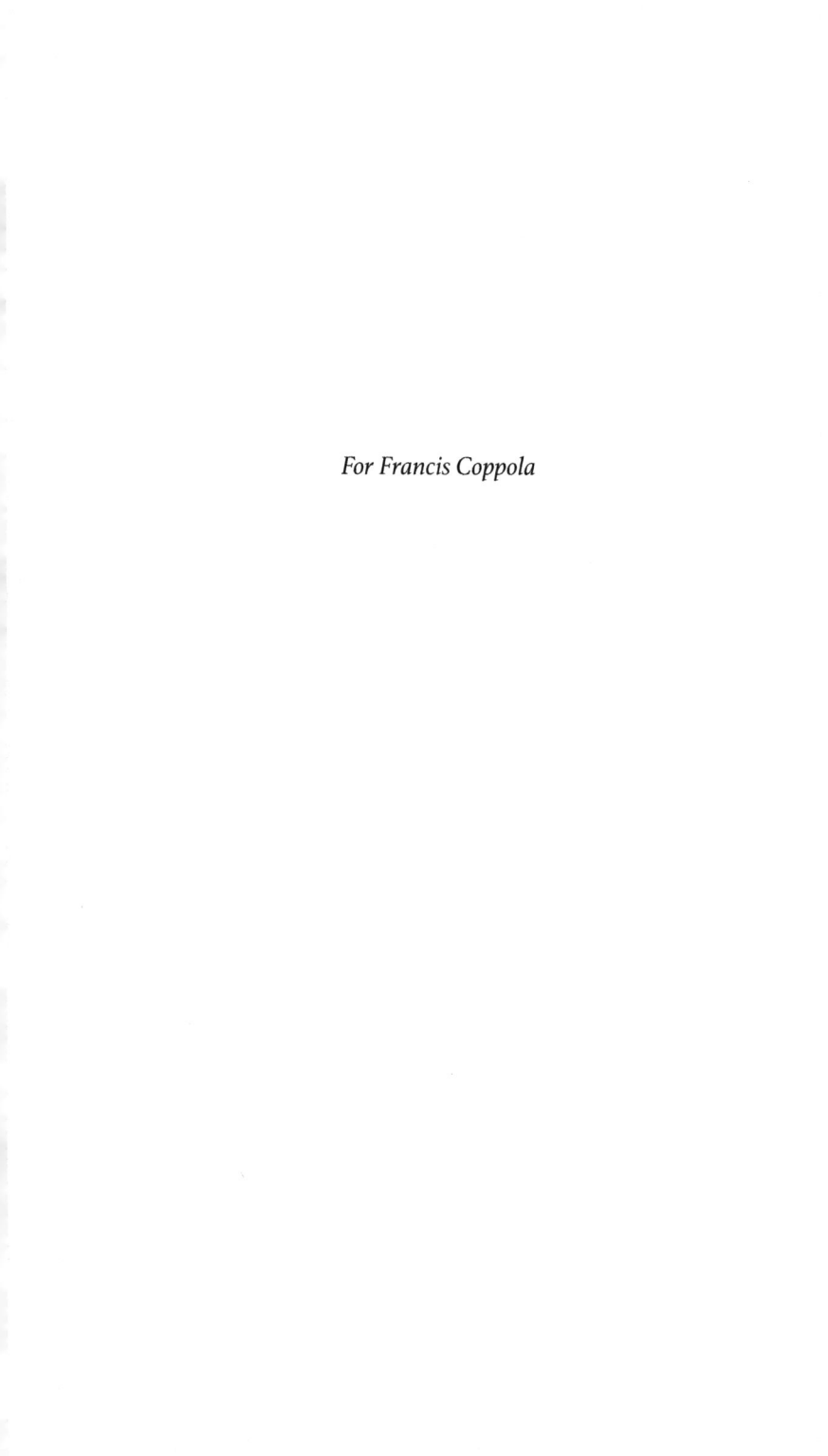

PART I

"A WOMAN LEFT LONELY"

1

The call from Anna Ryker came just before noon on a cloudy morning that promised much-needed rain. Horrendous fires had recently scorched Los Angeles and Santa Barbara counties after a long drought, making California a tinderbox ready to ignite at the careless drop of a cigarette or downed power line. Add in a minor earthquake that struck at 4:00 that morning, and SoCal residents woke up reminded of the fact we live in a precarious paradise. Yet it's a paradise from which we can't seem to tear ourselves away. So we clean up the mess any natural disaster leaves behind and do our best to push thoughts and fears of nature's capacity for destruction down into the deepest recesses of our minds. It's too much for most of us to face the possibility of ruination by something massive and out of our control. Instead, we let the more intimate crises break us down. The day-to-day terrors of life. I once read a phrase from a poet whose name I can't recall, but it has stayed with me: *The horrors of being human cripple us, not fears of the end of the world.*

I was about to be reminded of that fact.

"Dad, it's Doctor Ryker calling," my daughter yelled from the back deck. "She sounds upset."

"Did she say what was wrong?"

"No," Kathy said. "She tried to call your cell first, but you didn't pick up."

I took out my phone. The screen remained black even as I pressed the home button. The battery must have died while I worked patching a crack the late-night jolt had sent through the cinderblocks of my retaining wall. Branches of fallen red bougainvillea lay on the ground at my feet, entwined in splinters of thin white trellis slats, and crumbled cement that looked like fire ash was scattered across the green lawn. The small repair had kept me busy most of the morning.

I set down the spatula I held and closed the lid on a tub of crack filler. "Did Charley take off yet?" I asked.

"Twenty minutes ago."

I wiped my hands on a rag and went up on the patio, dabbing my finger on the tip of my seventeen-year-old daughter's nose as I passed her, nodded a *thank you,* then took the cordless phone from her hand.

"Anna, it's Jason," I said into the phone, stepping inside.

"I'm sorry to be so insistent," Anna replied. "I hope this isn't a bad time." Her voice sounded frightened and weak. Raspy, as well, as if she'd been yelling. Or crying.

"Not at all. What's up? Is everything okay?"

She inhaled sharply, a faint moan on her breath. "Could you come see me? I need ... I'd like to talk to you. I need your help. Something's happened. Something very bad."

I'd first met Anna during a murder case. As a psychiatrist, she'd treated the victim, Nora Lord. Over the course of several interviews, Anna provided me with useful information about Nora's life and the events that led to her death. By the end of the investigation, we'd become friends. More recently, she'd been helping my daughter deal with the trauma and aftermath of a violent abduction. Thanks to Anna's nurturing therapy, Kathy grows stronger every day. For that, I will eternally be in the doctor's debt.

Now, it seemed, she needed something from me.

The rain arrived as I left my house, growing to a downpour as I reached Topanga Canyon and maneuvered my way up the narrow, treacherous Horseshoe Lane to Anna's home. She lived near the top of the hill, in a charming, hippie-era structure that doubled as an office for her psychoanalytical practice. Her approach—a mixture of yoga and meditation with more traditional therapy techniques—was probably too unorthodox for anywhere but Los Angeles, and her house was equally unconventional: a cubist building painted orange and lime, with a wraparound porch and two entrances—one to her private residence, where she lived with her daughters, Janis and Billie, the other to her adjoining office. Today, its bright colors stood out in the grayness of the wet afternoon.

I parked by Anna's vintage Volvo, in the last curve of the road before a cul-de-sac would have forced me to head back down the hill. Looking up through my passenger window, I could see her silhouette just inside the screen of the kitchen door, a shadow in the darkness of the room. I jumped out of the car and darted up a long set of wooden stairs that dug into the hillside that was her front yard, rain pummeling down on me. Abstract sculptures lined the staircase, their metal glistening in the downpour. Chimes tinkled in the wind along the eaves of the house.

"Thank you for coming," she said, opening the screen

door. I hurried in, out of the torrent. The kitchen lights were off, the room gloomy. "What a mess outside." She reached into a counter drawer for a neatly folded towel and handed it to me, then watched me dry off through red, puffy eyes. Her hair was pulled into a haphazard ponytail and looked like it hadn't been washed in several days. Her skin was unusually pale. Even though she wore a thick beige sweater buttoned to her clavicle, her body trembled.

"Would you like some tea?" she asked.

"Sure. That would be great."

She nodded and turned to the counter beside the stove, busying herself dropping tea bags into mugs and pouring steaming water over them from a tin pot she lifted off the stove. Near her, rain pattered against the window glass, some of it sloshing onto the sill through a slightly opened bottom sash. Anna either didn't notice or didn't care, though she occasionally glanced its way as she worked. I sensed she didn't even see the window, or the rain, or anything outside, but rather something on her interior landscape—the thing that caused her such pain.

"Anna?" I said. "What is it? What's happened?"

Turning and catching me staring, whatever fragment of control she held onto vanished, and she burst into tears. The mug fell from her hand, shattering on the floor.

"Janis is dead," she whispered, the words floating out like the slow breath from a ghost. "Somebody killed her. Somebody butchered my little girl."

2

Ignoring the broken porcelain and spilled liquid, I stepped over and put my arms around Anna's shoulders. She didn't resist, but rather buried her head in my wet shirt and clung to me, as if she feared she might be sucked away into some void of grief if she let go. We stayed that way for a long while, her sobs almost rhythmic, like chants filling the cold, dark house.

"When did it happen?" I asked.

"Saturday night," she said, straightening up and wiping her eyes with the sleeve of the sweater. "Late. After midnight. I guess that makes it Sunday morning."

"Here, in the house?"

Anna nodded. "Billie found her." Billie was the younger daughter, at thirteen. Janis, the victim, was sixteen. I'd never met them, but my daughter had. She'd become friends with Janis over the past couple of months. "Stabbed to death in her bedroom," Anna said, struggling with the words. "Many times."

"Were you home?"

She pulled away from me, shaking her head, and sat on

a chair at the kitchen table. She perched on its edge, like she might jump up and flee the room at any moment. "No. I'd gone to a conference in Huntington Beach. It wasn't even something I cared about. I went with a friend, a colleague, who didn't want to drive down alone." Her eyes were so full of pain, I wondered how she was able even to speak. "If I'd stayed here ... If I'd never have gone ..."

"Don't do that," I said. "Don't blame yourself. There's nothing good down that road."

"I know. How many times have I said the same thing to my patients? We can't live our lives based on what *might* happen. And we can't blame ourselves for things out of our control that have." She looked around the dark room. "It feels like meaningless advice to me, now. I'm in alien territory."

I sat across from her at the table. "Tell me as much as you can."

"I'm still processing it all myself."

"I understand. Take your time."

"Our neighbor, Marty ... You met him, remember? Marty Astor." She pointed at a second kitchen door that led to the backyard. "He lives up above us with his husband, Lenny DeWitt." I nodded. "They're such sweet people. Marty spotted Billie wandering on the street that night. He brought her home. Then he called me and told me I needed to come back immediately. He wouldn't give any details. I guess he didn't want to scare me too much before making such a long drive. But not knowing was the most terrifying thing of all. I raced all the way here. Eighty, ninety miles an hour. It's a miracle I wasn't killed." She closed her eyes. "God, what a selfish thing to say."

With this, she started again to cry. I grabbed a roll of paper towels from the counter, pulled several loose, and handed them to her. "It's not selfish," I said, "If something had happened to you, Billie would be all alone."

She nodded, wiping her eyes, then stared at the wadded paper in her hand.

"Did Marty contact the police?" I asked.

"Yes. And he stayed with Billie until they arrived. They were all waiting for me when I got here."

"Who are the investigating officers? Do you remember their names?"

She stood, pensive, and went over to a small desk under a wall-mounted phone. "There were two detectives, but I only got a card from one." She searched around a bit, through papers and notebooks, until she found a business card that she brought back to me. It was standard LAPD issue: the shield logo on the left side, the officer's name and rank in the center, his contact information in the lower right corner. The detective's name was Dante Caruso. I knew him; our paths had crossed when separate investigations intersected—one LAPD, the other Sheriff's Homicide, my old department.

"I suppose it would be too much to hope they already had a suspect in custody," I said.

Anna didn't answer. She stared silently at the broken tea mug and spilled liquid on the floor. Outside, the wind slammed rain pellets against the side of the house, and the wood beams within the walls creaked and groaned as if the house itself ached along with Anna. "I should clean up the mess," she said.

I reached over and put a hand on her shoulder, stopping her from rising. "Let me."

I stooped down to recover the shards of broken porcelain and dropped them into a trash can under the sink, then used a hand broom and dust bin to sweep up the smaller slivers that remained. I unspooled a length of the paper towel and blotted up the spilled tea.

"She was stabbed ten times," Anna said. "With a large knife, taken from here in the kitchen." She pointed to a wood block on the counter. Several carving knifes of varying sizes protruded from its slanted top. There was a noticeable space where the largest should have been.

"Do the police have the weapon in their possession?" I said.

"Billie was holding it when Marty found her. She must have picked it up, taken it for some crazy reason, when she discovered Janis's body." Urgency crept into Anna's voice. "She was in shock. That's the only thing that makes sense, right? She came home, found Janis, probably embraced her to try and revive her. That's why she had blood all over her hands and clothes."

I sat back down in my chair, reacting to the news that Billie had been covered in blood when Marty found her. Realization sank in. "They've arrested her, haven't they?"

Anna put her hand to her mouth and closed her eyes as another wave of sobs overwhelmed her. "It's like one of those horrible dreams in which you feel conscious but can't escape the nightmare. Lucid dreams, we call them."

"Do you want a drink of water? Something stronger?"

She shook her head. "Just give me a moment." She lowered her head. Her shoulders shuddered. I watched her, heartbroken, tense, and a little anxious. As the facts trickled out, I had a strong idea where this all was going. "The detectives seem so certain of her guilt," she said. "But they're rushing to judgment. It's impossible to think Billie could ... She's not capable of something so horrific." Her eyes cleared of their sadness, replaced by the fire of desperation. "I need your help, Jason. You're the only one I can turn to. I need you to find my baby's killer. I need you to prove the police are wrong and save my daughter."

Anna's request instantly troubled me. First, because I was no longer a cop. I'd handed in my badge and gun months ago, taking an indefinite leave of absence from the sheriff's department. I wasn't sure when, or if, I'd go back. And I'd never considered working as a private investigator. Now Anna was asking me to launch a separate inquiry, one she hoped would find evidence that called into question the judgment of two seasoned LAPD detectives. Agreeing to help her would put me on the path of a potential landmine. Conversely, the idea that a thirteen-year-old girl could brutally murder her sixteen-year-old sister seemed unimaginable, and it disturbed me that the detectives had, in one night, decided to arrest her.

"Are the police holding her?" I asked.

"No. The judge remanded her into my care this morning."

"So she's home. Good. What is she saying happened?"

Anna seemed not to want to answer the question. She asked, "Will you help us?"

"Anna, I don't know. You've taken me by surprise with the request."

"You could launch your own investigation, couldn't you? A private one. There's no law against it, as far as I can ascertain. You're a free agent now that you're out of the sheriff's department, so it's not an issue of jurisdiction."

She'd obviously done some research. "I'm not a licensed private eye," I said. "I'm a civilian. That would make a private investigation illegal here in California. And I'd be working in contradiction to an official LAPD investigation, which is tricky for all kinds of reasons."

"The detectives are wrong," Anna said. "Or they don't

care. I think they're just being lazy. They want the easiest solution so they can go move on."

I doubted this was true. The idea that cops sloppily put cases together in a hurried effort to close them and move on is the stuff of bad movies. More times than not, they're careful and thorough. Nobody wants to send an innocent person to jail. And nobody wants a guilty one to walk on a technicality. "Look at the evidence they have in front of them," I said. "If they've made a mistake, it's not out of laziness. I urge you to give them another forty-eight hours. At the least. Let them do what they know how to do."

"They've arrested an innocent young girl! *My* little girl!" She pulled back, closing her eyes and taking a few deep breaths, working to rein in her fury. "I'm sorry. I know anger is counterproductive." She exhaled through an open mouth that formed a perfect circle. "But Billie is innocent. Please, help me prove that. There's no one else I can ask. No one else to turn to."

"What does Billie say happened that night?" I asked again.

"Nothing. She hasn't spoken a word since I got back from Huntington Beach. She stays in bed and stares at the wall. She won't eat. Won't even look at me when I come into the room. It's been two days. I've tried every technique I know. I can't get through to her."

"She's in shock," I said. "It's disturbing to see a dead body, even for an adult. I've never become immune to it, and I've seen more than my share." I didn't say—even as I considered it—that her condition might also stem from guilt over a horrible and violent action. As hard as it was for me to imagine such a display of violence, I knew the world was marred by horrible, inexplicable behavior, often from the most unlikely people. It was one of the reasons I'd had a job for as long as I did. "Talk to me about Billie's state when Marty found her."

"Bewildered, according to him. Disoriented. He said she wouldn't answer his questions. Once he was sure the blood wasn't her own from some wound, he brought her back here. The front door was wide open, he said, but Billie wouldn't go inside. She acted like she was terrified of the house. Or of something in it. Marty didn't push. They sat on the front porch. He asked her where I was. He couldn't get her to say anything. Finally, he came inside to look around. And he found Janis."

"Was Janis home all night?" I asked.

"I don't know. Her plans for the evening were vague when I spoke with her before I left for Huntington Beach. She told me she might go to the movies with her friend, Isabelle, or she might just stay in and work on a school project that was due next week."

"Did the police talk to Isabelle?"

"Yes. She told them Janis canceled the movie plans at the last minute."

"Did she say why?"

"Isabelle didn't know."

"What about Billie? What did she do all evening?"

"She went to a party at a friend's house down the road. She'd planned to stay the night."

"But she didn't. Why not?"

"Her friend, Caitlyn, said Billie felt ill," Anna said. "She went to lie down for a bit, but it didn't help, so she came home."

"What time did she leave the party?"

"Around eleven-thirty. Maybe midnight."

"And the coroner placed time of death when?"

"Between midnight and two a.m."

"How far from here is the house where this party took place?" I assumed it must be close. Billie couldn't drive yet.

"A five-minute walk," Anna said. "But there's no way to confirm she came straight home. Or what time she really left the party. Maybe it was after midnight. And it was certainly after the murder. Marty didn't come across her in the street until around two-thirty."

But she'd obviously gone home first. He found her covered in blood. Holding a knife. *The* knife. Whoever killed Janis could have done it in a matter of minutes. Seconds, even, if there was little or no struggle.

"I assume the crime scene unit did a bloodstain pattern analysis," I said. Stabbing a victim creates a specific pattern on the hands or gloves of the attacker. The spatter test is kind of like a gunshot residue test—though not as reliable. Still, the results would have factored into the decision to arrest.

"It was inconclusive," Anna said. "Billie had already wiped her hands on her clothes, disturbing any pattern there might have been."

"Did the police find blood anywhere else in the house?"

"A little bit. In the girls' sink. They share a bathroom. A drop or two at the mouth of the drain."

This raised a question in my mind, one I'd want to ask the detectives, if I took this further.

If I took this any further. Was I even considering it?

I got up and removed a drinking glass from the cupboard, filled it with tap water, then set it down in front of Anna. Anna glanced at it but left it untouched.

"I know Billie can hear and see," she said, "even if she's unable to speak. She's aware of what's going on. And I'm certain it's making things worse. Pushing her deeper into her own darkness and silence."

"Perhaps you should have someone else talk to her. Another psychiatrist. Someone she doesn't know. Maybe they would have better luck getting through to her."

"Because Billie is afraid to tell me what happened? Is that what you're implying?"

"You have to consider all possibilities here, Anna. I don't mean to sound cold. And I don't want to scare you."

"She's innocent. I have no doubt in my mind. Not because she's my daughter, but because I know her. The kind of girl she is. What she's capable of."

I didn't respond. All of what she was saying, I knew, would be colored by the fact that she *was* Billie's mother.

"I've put you in a horrible position, haven't I?" she said.

"I'm glad you called me. And I want to support you the best way I can. As a friend."

"Will you at least look at Janis's room? Maybe you'll notice something the police missed."

I was unable to further let her down by saying no.

3

It was a typical teen girl's room, not much different from my Kathy's domain. A blue-and-maroon swirl-pattern rug covered half of the hardwood floor. Bunched up and wrinkled clothes lay on it and on the backs of chairs. The walls were light pink, the desk and bookcase clean white. The bookshelves contained YA paperbacks, a few stuffed animals, a cheap record player, and a small collection of vinyl LPs. Posters of singers and bands—Beyoncé, Imagine Dragons, Sam Smith—hung above a desk cluttered with schoolbooks, magazines, pens and markers, nail polish bottles, and framed photographs: Janis with her friends, with her mom, with her sister. She appeared flamboyant, smiling and laughing, always on, always posing.

A happy life cut short.

Billie, to the contrary, looked subdued and uncomfortable in every picture. She mostly dressed in black, with matching hair that made her pale skin stand out. I remember my daughter telling me Janis was the wild one while Billie was an introvert. "A total goth," Kathy had called her.

The bed sat between two windows. A framed copy of the LP cover to Janis Joplin's *Pearl* album was centered on the wall above its headboard. I remembered Anna telling me she'd named Janis after the singer. (Billie had been named for Billie Holiday.) On the album cover, the rock icon sat on a vintage loveseat wearing red pants and a multicolored top, with a pink boa wrapped up in her hair. I thought of a song from the album, "A Woman Left Lonely." That was Anna. Left lonely. Distraught. Terrified.

The frame's glass covering, and the wall around it, was dappled with blood. Blankets and sheets cascaded over the bed's bottom edge, exposing a mattress at the center of which a crimson stain formed a dark oval. More blood speckled the white lamp shade on the nightstand. Even without the body present, I knew from the pattern of blood that rage had propelled this attack. It was the work of an individual who'd lost control, acting with little concern for the death fluids that surely covered him or her. The butcher had arced the knife high before each vicious plunge.

I turned in place, eyeballing the room, looking to see if, as Anna hoped, something stood out: a little piece of overlooked evidence that could send the investigation in a new and different direction, away from Billie and toward another assailant. But other than the stain on the bed and the blood on the walls, everything seemed normal and ordinary. A once bright, cheerful, comfortingly chaotic room, now marred forever by violence and loss.

Anna sat on the edge of Billie's bed in the room across the hall. Her daughter lay on her side, silent and still as her mother massaged fingers through the girl's jet-black hair. Billie stared at the wall, eyes glazed over, skin as pale as white paper. Anna sang softly what sounded like a lullaby. She was so caught up in the song—and in her daughter—it took a moment for her to sense my presence. When she did, she looked up at me with urgency and anticipation. I motioned for her to follow, then turned and left the room.

In the kitchen, I drank from the glass of water Anna had left untouched, and I looked out the window into the backyard, gazing up the hill toward the house where Marty lived with Lenny. I remembered the couple. Marty was a writer with a warm soul. Lenny, a painter and a sculptor, was more reserved and distrustful. It was his artwork that lined Anna's front lawn steps.

"So?" Anna said from the doorway.

I set the glass down and turned to her. "Whoever did this to Janis had a lot of rage going on inside," I said. "Did she have any enemies?"

"Not that kind. At least not to my knowledge. The usual trouble a sixteen-year-old has with other girls at school, of course. Envy. Competition. I'm sure Kathy has gone through the same. But enemies capable of this? No."

"What was the dynamic between the sisters?"

Anna tensed at the question. "They loved each other. Very much."

"In the family photos I saw in Janis's room, Billie seems very sad. Withdrawn, even."

"She's a troubled child. I won't deny that. Her father's death hit her very hard." I knew Anna's husband had died in a car accident several years ago. "That doesn't make her a killer."

"I'm not saying it does. And please don't take my questions and comments the wrong way. I'm simply trying to construct a portrait."

"Should I feel optimistic?"

"My advice stands," I said. "Let the cops do their job. At least give them a few more days. If this were my case, and I didn't know you, I would have made the same call. I'm sorry if that's hard for you to hear."

"Billie is thirteen, for God's sake," Anna said, as if this was the only attestation needed.

"The last thing any detective wants to do is put an innocent young girl behind bars. They also know how hard this is for you, even if they don't show it."

Her energy withered. "I'm sorry. I don't mean to snap."

"Anna, you owe me no apologies."

"I don't know how to react to any of this, other than to be terrified." She crossed her arms over her chest. "I've never feared my own death. I've accepted its inevitability. Death as part of life. The natural end to our time and purpose here on earth. But I've never imagined outliving one of my children. Now Janis is gone. I refuse to lose the other because the police made a mistake. So I called you. But if you can't help us, I understand."

"I need to think about this," I said. "You need to give me some time."

"Billie may not have much."

"Just until tomorrow. I'll discuss things with Charley and Kathy. I'll give you an answer in the morning, I promise."

Anna nodded, a feeble smile softening her expression; it was not surprising she'd take any bit of hope that came along in the jetsam and flotsam of this tragedy.

We said our goodbyes on the porch. In the time I'd been with her, a little over an hour, the rain had stopped. I made my way down to the car. Glancing back, I saw she still stood where I'd left her, gazing off to the west where the sky had cleared. The sun was about to disappear behind the mountains of Malibu, on its way down into the sea, but for Anna and Billie Ryker, night had already come.

I drove home listening to *Hard Candy*, a Counting Crows album about memory, failure, and regret, and I pondered Anna's difficult, heart-wrenching request. The thought that Billie might be capable of such a heinous act of violence disturbed me in ways I found hard to even contemplate.

I've usually looked at evil as mostly a learned condition, picked up by perpetrators after a lifetime of witnessing vicious behavior and the violent acts of others: abusive parents, bullying children, predatory family members—something taught, like bigotry or misogyny. Christianity holds that much, if not all, of the malevolence in the world originates as a force outside our natural selves. Lucifer. Satan. The Devil. Still others believe the tendency toward violence is an inherent malady carried in our DNA from birth.

Over the course of the next days and weeks, it would become increasingly hard for me to dismiss this final thesis, that violent evil is deep-rooted and intrinsic, growing inside a handful of us, unstoppable, simply waiting to be let loose.

4

When I returned home, I didn't see Charley's car out front, and I assumed this meant she was still at her burn therapy session. Charlotte "Charley" Frasier, the woman I live with and love, had been severely injured recently, the result of an explosion and subsequent fire caused by a man who'd wanted to kill us both. The fire damaged the flesh of Charley's left arm, shoulder, part of her neck, and her lower face. The wounds require extensive medication and skin grafting, subjecting her to painful therapy sessions, twice a week, with a burn specialist. She'd been scheduled for something called debridement today, a surgical process to remove necrotic tissue from the injured sites to promote the growth of healthy replacement.

She'd refused to let me accompany her—as was the case with all the sessions ("This is my journey, Jagger," she said, using the nickname she'd been calling me for as long as I've known her, too many years to count). And she rarely discussed with me what happens while she is there. I worry the silence and distance comes from a deeper place: a shame over her physical condition. And perhaps there is a part of her that blames me for the disfigurement. It had been my obsessive tracking of a deranged ex-cop connected to my past that spurred the attack and led to her debilitation. She had every right to point a finger, and all her anger, at me.

Kathy *was* home; the walls of the house reverberated with the thumping energy of Childish Gambino, coming from speakers in her room. I had to pound over it when I knocked on her door. The music softened and she said, "Yeah?"

"Okay to come in?"

"Enter."

My daughter sat on the floor, her back against the bed, a laptop computer in front of her open to a Pinterest page.

"Everything okay with Doctor Ryker?" she asked.

"You might want to turn the music off and close your computer."

Once she had, I told her about Janis.

"Oh my God," Kathy said, wide-eyed, sitting forward. "I just saw her last week, when I went to my session with Doctor Ryker."

"This took place early Sunday morning."

"What happened to her?"

"She was stabbed to death in her bedroom," I said. "A neighbor discovered Billie wandering the street afterward, covered in blood and carrying the murder weapon, a knife."

"Whoa. They don't think she killed Janis, do they?"

"Until another suspect comes along, she's their focus. They've arrested her."

"She's fucking thirteen," Kathy blurted out, then quickly caught herself. "Sorry. But come on. Are they serious?"

I didn't answer, but looked around the space, eerily reminded of Janis's bedroom as I took in the posters on Kathy's wall, the clothes strewn haphazardly here and there, the desk cluttered with homework. The mess, the disarray was in Kathy's case a good thing. For weeks after her abduction, she'd been obsessive in her neatness and personal control, to the point of neurosis: constantly straightening things up, washing her hands every hour, taking at least two showers a day. More recently, she'd seemed to regain her balance, to relax and get messy again. She'd done this with the help of Anna Ryker.

Looking at my daughter now, a selfish realization I'd not considered until this moment came to me: Anna's situation —her nightmare—would no doubt take her away from her practice, leaving patients like Kathy unmoored. It was inevitable and as it should be; Anna needed to take as much time as necessary to deal with the horror and heal from her loss. As a father, though, I couldn't help but wonder what this might do to my own daughter's delicate recovery.

"Wow," Kathy said. "I can't believe this. You just never know, do you?"

"No, Katbird, you don't."

"The poor woman. Should I call? Give my condolences?"

"Maybe in a few days. She's a mess right now."

"I'm sure. And *Billie*. That poor little girl." Kathy frowned. "Why did Doctor Ryker want to see you?"

"She asked me to launch a private investigation to prove Billie's innocence."

"Oh. That makes sense. Good idea." When I didn't respond, she gave me a curious look. "You're gonna do it, right?"

"I don't know yet. I'm not even sure I could. I'm on leave

from the department. And it's not the sheriff's department's jurisdiction if I was still working."

"Is there a law against a private citizen investigating a criminal case?"

"In California, it's illegal for one to work as an investigator. And I don't have a license as a private eye."

"I bet that law just applies to getting paid for it, no?"

"I'm not sure. I'd have to see."

"Or get a license. Should be a piece of cake for you."

"Sounds like you really want me to do this."

"Dad, we owe Doctor Ryker so much. If you can help her, I think you should." She paused. "Unless you think Billie's guilty?"

"I don't have enough information to make that call."

"Doesn't Anna deserve to know, one way or the other?"

"Yes," I said, "she does."

IN MY STUDY, I TURNED ON MY LAPTOP AND DID A SEARCH FOR articles about Janis Ryker's murder. There were two paragraphs in the crime watch section of the LA Times and another in the Daily News. Brief blurbs—*teenage daughter of Topanga Canyon psychoanalyst brutally murdered in her home*—nothing more. No mention of Billie as a suspect, only as the victim's younger sister. Caruso had somehow managed to keep her arrest from the media. Not an easy feat, and I applauded him for pulling it off. I knew from experience it wouldn't hold for long, but the fact he'd tried reinforced my belief that Caruso was not acting imprudently with the investigation. He wasn't trying to make a splash with a quick arrest. He and his partner had done what they felt they had to, given the evidence in front of them. As I told Anna, I would have done the same.

I took his card from my pocket and stared at it. I remembered Dante as a decent detective, smart and hardworking, the kind who wouldn't make rash decisions about a murder case simply to be done with it. He also was the kind of man who wouldn't take too kindly to an unemployed homicide detective questioning his judgment. If I decided to reach out to him, I'd have to tread carefully.

WHEN CHARLEY CAME HOME AN HOUR LATER, SHE LOOKED troubled and in pain, her eyes red. She had fresh bandages on her neck and one cheek. There was some spotting on the gauze that covered the burn wounds.

"Don't ask me how it went," she said, breezing past me as she headed into the kitchen. "And don't get nervous. The blood spotting is normal." She opened the fridge and took out a bottle of cranberry juice, filled a glass with some, then chased down an Advil with a gulp. "She can only do so much at a time," Charley said, referring to her doctor. "I've got to go back in four days for more. Yippee for me." She set down the glass. "Don't worry." She grabbed my hand. "This is the worst part. It'll be over soon. I won't be an angry, bitter bitch forever."

"You can be angry and bitter for as long as you want," I said.

"Stop. Don't humor me. And I don't want to talk about it anymore."

"Then we won't."

At the close of the case that put her in the hospital (and caused me to take an extended break from the career I'd had for over a decade), I'd asked Charley to marry me. She'd said yes. We'd not made plans beyond that. She didn't want to rush into anything, needing to heal first. I tried to ignore the gnawing fear that she might, over the course of that healing period, change her mind.

"How was *your* day?" she asked, leading me out the patio door and onto the back deck. "You finished patching the wall, I see." She pointed to my handiwork across the lawn.

"Still gotta paint and clean up the mess on the ground."

"What's the phrase, well begun is half done?"

"If you say so."

"Did you run out of steam?"

"No, I got called away." I told her about Anna's call, and about Janis Ryker. "It's horrible, Charley. I took a look at the crime scene. I've seen a lot of bad ones over the years, but this one cuts deep. And close."

"My God. The poor woman. Who caught the case?"

"LAPD. Remember a guy named Dante Caruso?"

"Vaguely."

"He and someone I don't know are the lead detectives."

"Any reason to think they don't know what they're doing?"

"Not a single one."

"So, what are you going to tell Anna?"

"I don't know. Any suggestions?"

"No, and I wouldn't give one, even if I had it," Charley said. "Not on this. You made the choice to step away. If you want to go back in, it's gotta be your call and not because I told you I thought you should."

"Do you think I should?"

She laughed, wagging an admonishing finger.

"You gotta give me something," I said.

"Okay. I'll say this much. I don't get the feeling you're too happy having nothing to do."

"I've plenty to do," I said, motioning toward the repaired retaining wall.

"Then I guess I'm mistaken. Tell Anna no, then go clean up the broken bougainvillea and cinderblock."

It's always disturbing when someone knows you better than you know yourself.

5

Anna called in the middle of the night, the sound and the light from my cell phone disturbing the silence and darkness of our bedroom. Charley moaned and shifted her position, turning her back to me and curling up, but not waking. I picked up my cell and crept out to the backyard deck. Crickets chirped. A fine mist hung in the air. The moon was a pale hook above the trees.

"I know it's late," Anna said. "I'm sorry."

"It's fine, Anna. What's going on?" I closed the sliding door behind me.

"I went in to check on Billie a little while ago. She was sleeping restlessly, bathed in sweat. She muttered something in her sleep. It sounded like, 'Why not?'"

"What do you think it means?"

"I don't know."

"Is it normal for someone in her silent state to speak while sleeping?"

"There are no hard and fast rules to catatonic shock or depression. It doesn't necessarily indicate a returning to normal."

"Then I'm not sure why you're telling me." As I spoke, I glanced over at the patio door. Charley stood barely visible in the darkness of the living room, looking curiously at me and frowning. "Is there anything I can do?" I asked Anna.

"I'm sorry. I shouldn't have called. I guess I—"

"Wanted an excuse," I said, finishing the phrase for her. "You want to know what I've decided."

"See? You are a good detective." I wanted to believe she smiled a bit as she said this.

"Anna, what you're going through is horrendous. I wish I could agree to help you without thought or hesitation. But the request is complicated, filled with all kinds of legal and ethical pitfalls. You've got to give me time to think them through."

"I understand," she said, though I sensed she didn't, not really. "You need to do what you have to do." The last phrase sounded laced with condescension. Maybe that was just my erroneous reading of her tone, done out of guilt.

"We'll talk in the morning," I said. "Try and get some rest. Goodnight." I ended the call and went back inside. "That was Anna Ryker," I told Charley. "Billie said something in her sleep. Anna wanted to believe it meant something."

"So she called you at this hour?"

"She's desperate. She wants me to help her and she's having trouble accepting the possibility that I might say no."

"But you won't say no. You've already decided, even if you don't know it yet. That's why you answered the call at two in the morning."

"Let's go back to bed."

"Jagger, why make her suffer? Call her back. Tell her you'll do it. Maybe then at least she'll be able to get a decent night's sleep."

I looked down at the phone in my hand and debated. Despite Charley's certainty, I was not ready to commit. Maybe I feared I couldn't deliver. Or perhaps I was scared I might discover something none of us wanted to learn.

The next morning, Kathy told me about a strange dream she'd had the night before. "You're going to think I'm crazy," she said, "but I'm pretty sure it means something."

"Sounds intriguing," I said. We were sitting at the kitchen table. She ate yogurt. I drank coffee.

"I know I've had a lot of them since my abduction. Dreams."

"More than anyone could ever want, I'm sure."

"Yeah. And they've always been about me. At least the ones I remember. And about the guy who took me."

She referred to JoJo Sellers, a predator of women who'd taken Kathy hostage and raped her during a murder case I'd investigating that connected to a private Hollywood sex club. I shot and killed the man during her rescue.

"This one was different," Kathy said. "For the first time, I didn't dream about myself. I dreamed about Janis."

I set my cup down and leaned forward. "Go on."

"We were together, on the rooftop of some tall building downtown," Kathy said. "There was a strange event going on. Makeshift, like a pop-up party. Beach chairs and folding tables. A DJ was playing old songs. Zeppelin. The kids were all teenagers, my age and younger, and they were dancing to it. Janis had on red pants, bell bottoms. Her hair was tied up with a big pink plume boa."

An image of the album cover for *Pearl* that hung on Janis's wall came to mind. "Have you ever been in Janis's room?" I asked.

"Twice, yeah. And I know. It's the same outfit as on that album cover. So yeah, maybe that's where I got the image."

"One never knows about the subconscious," I said.

"In the dream, Janis kept yelling at the DJ to stop playing Led Zeppelin. 'No more fucking Zeppelin,' she screamed. 'It's killing me! I hate Jimmy Page! I want Jagger!' It seemed weird that Janis used Charley's nickname for you."

"*She* didn't," I said. "Your subconscious did."

"Whatever. You know what I mean. It was also odd, because Page is a guitar player and Jagger a singer. So there's that contradiction." She took a spoonful of yogurt. "Anyway, Janis seemed really angry. The DJ just laughed and waved her off. He turned the music up, too loud. It was a song called 'Custard Pie.'"

"From *Physical Graffiti*," I said.

Kathy shrugged. "If you say so. It got really distorted coming out of the speakers. When Janis looked at me, I saw tears in her eyes. Then she turned and ran across the rooftop and did a swan dive over the edge. I hurried after her and looked down. She was gone. No sign of her at all." Kathy paused, and then said, "That's all I remember."

"She's clearly on your mind. The Joplin reference is obvious. So is the Jagger one. You had this dream after I told you Anna wanted me to launch an investigation."

"There's something else, but I'm not sure I can explain it so it'll make sense," Kathy said. "The dream didn't feel like it was *mine*. Until last night, mine always had a certain feeling. A recurring vibe. Last night, though, the colors in the dream were way different than usual. Special. Stronger. More intense. The sounds, too. All unlike anything I can remember ever experiencing in a dream."

"That could be intentional," I said. Kathy looked at me, confused. "I wouldn't be surprised if your subconscious decided to change the game on you. To move away from what you're used to and take you into a new realm. A symbol that you're finally starting to let go. This could just be another part of the healing."

"Interesting theory, Doctor Dad, but I have another one."

"Okay."

"Promise you won't say it sounds stupid, even if you think it does."

"Some of my best deductions seemed stupid when I first considered them."

"What if Janis is reaching out to me? Like she's trying to tell me something about how she died. And why."

"Hmm," I said.

"What does that mean?"

"As Bogie said in *The Big Sleep,* it means *hmm.*"

"You don't believe me."

"That she's reaching out to you in dreams, as a spirit or ghost? In this instance, no, I don't."

"Why not? Who are we to dismiss the idea of a supernatural world? I don't, even if I have no firsthand experience."

"I'm not saying I dismiss the supernatural. I just don't believe ghosts can solve cases."

"Spoken like a true skeptic," Charley said, entering. She'd taken the bandages from the night before off her face to allow the damaged epidermis to breathe. The new skin emerging beneath was red and vibrant, as if freshly slapped. "I know, I look like the poster for a horror movie. But the cool air feels good."

"You look beautiful," I said.

Charley rolled her eyes and poured herself some coffee. "What's with the ghost talk?"

"Kathy had a dream about Janis Ryker. She thinks Janis's ghost may be trying to contact her."

"I simply posited the theory," Kathy said.

"She's accusing me of arrogance," I said, "because she thinks I dismiss the supernatural. Which, by the way, I don't."

"I never said you were arrogant."

"Kathy, I'm with you," Charley said. "Who are we to say something doesn't exist simply because we've had no contact or experience with it?"

"Guys, I'm not dismissing the existence of another world." I said. "I just think, in this case, you're dealing with an active subconscious mind, nothing else."

"Keep a record of your dreams going forward," Charley told Kathy.

"Good idea," Kathy said. She took out her phone and started writing something in her notes app.

Charley sipped coffee and looked at me, as if waiting for me to say something. When I didn't, she said, "Did you call Anna back?"

"No. I feel I should talk to her about it, face-to-face."

"You're going up there again?"

I nodded, asked if she wanted to go along.

Charley shook her head. "This is your issue," she said. "I don't want to be intrusive. I don't even know the woman. Whatever you tell her, and however she reacts, is something between the two of you."

THE SUN WAS OUT, THE DAY WARM AND DRY, BUT ANNA'S house looked darker inside than it had the day before in the rain. It took several minutes and many loud knocks for her to answer. Her physical condition had deteriorated in the twenty-some hours since I'd last seen her: hair matted with sweat, skin now a sickly gray, eyes red and swollen from too many tears. She seemed aware of this, too, and embarrassed; she kept her head down as she let me into the kitchen.

"Have you been out there long?" she asked. "I must have dozed off. I had trouble sleeping last night after I called you. Again, sorry about that."

"You need rest. Maybe you should take something to help."

"No." She practically barked out the word. "I don't want to be asleep when Billie comes back to me."

I nodded. "How is she?"

"No change. I've asked her physician to arrange for an IV. She's not eating or drinking. I'm scared."

"Do you have a friend who can stay with you?"

"Don't worry about me," she said. "Have you come to a decision?"

"Yes. It's not exactly what you want, but I'm willing to make you a deal."

"Okay ..."

"I've worked with one of the detectives handling the case," I said. "Dante Caruso. He's a decent man and a good detective. I'll talk to him. And I promise to approach the meeting with a healthy amount of skepticism. If I find any fault with his take on things, any lapse in judgment, or any reason to suspect he is sloppily rushing an arrest through, I'll do what you're asking. If, conversely, after speaking with him, I'm convinced you're wrong about his motives and the way he's handling the investigation, you need to agree to give him more time." I was adding to her confusion and hated that fact, but it was the only course I could comfortably take.

"Okay," she said. "I'll take what I can get."

"Good."

Someone knocked on the door.

"Please tell whoever it is that I'm unavailable." She turned her back to the door and stared out the window over the sink, onto a backyard awash in sunlight.

"We could simply ignore them," I said.

"I'm sure they know we're here. I don't want to be rude." There was no anger or sarcasm in her tone. She sounded genteel.

"As you wish." I stepped to the door and cracked it open.

Anna's neighbor, Martin Astor—the one who'd found Billie wandering the streets covered in blood after Janis's murder—stood on the porch, looking pretty much the same as he had when I'd first met him, years before. He may even have been wearing the same clothes: a white T-shirt with a red peace symbol on its front, wrinkled khaki pants, black and white Converse low-tops that looked at least ten years old. He'd changed his glasses from round metallic John Lennon frames to black plastic Buddy Holly ones. This gave him a trendy nerd-look. His belly was a little larger, his hair a little grayer. The strands that hung down to his neck were damp from either sweat or a recent shower. His bald top had a red, sunburned glow.

"Detective, I'm so glad you're here," he said, pushing open the door and giving me a bearhug. "She's barely keeping it together," he whispered in my ear. "I'm worried about her." He let go and hurried past me to Anna, grabbing her even more ferociously. "Did you get some sleep? You must be famished. I brought food." He released her from his grip, spun on his toes, and rushed back out to the porch. There he picked up two large blue and white lunch boxes he'd left at the top of the steps. "Lenny's Lasagna." He smiled, lifting the boxes high. "Your favorite. And my specialty, caprese salad with fresh basil from our garden."

"Marty, you didn't have to do this," Anna said. "I have plenty in the fridge. Thank you, though."

"It's not the *having*, honey, it's the *fixing*," Marty said. "That's what wears you out. Am I right, Detective? Besides, you know how much we love to cook." He put the containers in the refrigerator, rearranging items inside to make room. "You're here to help, aren't you?" he said to me as he worked. "I know how things look. But I also know Billie. I watched that girl grow up. I've seen how much she loves her sister, even when she's acting like she hates her. Billie doesn't have that kind of anger inside, not to do something so—" He stopped himself and glanced at Anna, remorseful that he'd almost let slip a callous comment. She seemed not to notice; I don't think she was paying attention. She focused on rubbing behind the ears of a black and white cat that had jumped up on the counter.

"May I sit with Billie a bit?" I said. "Talk to her?"

Anna looked at me, gratitude brightening her face. "Of course."

Billie's eyes were closed, her forehead and hair slick with sweat. A thick blanket covered her, pulled all the way up to her neck. Music played softly from a small speaker connected to an iPad on her desk, a hauntingly edgy song called "Day of the Lords" from *Unknown Pleasures*, an old album by Joy Division. They'd made only two albums when the band's lead singer, Ian Curtis—who suffered from epilepsy and severe depression—committed suicide.

"I've been playing the music I know she likes," Anna said as we stood in the doorway to Billie's bedroom. Marty had remained in the kitchen to heat up some food for Anna, wanting to give us private time with the young girl. "Most of it's dark goth stuff. Maybe that's a mistake."

"I suspect anything that might make her feel comfortable is a good thing," I said. "And as for dark goth stuff, it doesn't get much darker, or better, than Joy Division." This provoked a weak smile from Anna.

"That's a whole side of Billie I don't understand. She's never really let me in."

She crossed over to the desk, turned the music down so that it was barely audible but still present, then sat in a chair she kept beside the bed.

"Hi, sweetie," Anna said. "This is Jason, a good friend. He's Kathy's father. Do you remember her? She comes to see me for help. Janis and she are friends."

I noted her intentional use of the present tense in referring to Janis. A protective action. She wasn't talking to Billie about Janis's murder, though the young girl obviously had witnessed it (and perhaps been responsible). I understood the logic; if the trauma of her sister's death drove Billie to this dark and silent place, reminding her of it might keep her there.

As Anna spoke, I studied the young girl, looking for any signs of awareness. Billie barely moved, not even a twitch of the eye—just the slow, steady rise and fall of her torso as she breathed. If she was faking this state of shock and withdrawal, she was damned good at the play-acting. If real, then who knew how long she'd remain there, or if she'd ever return.

6

That afternoon, I met with Dante Caruso at Terry's Bar and Grill on Grand Avenue downtown, a favorite of the police station and city hall crowd. A dozen or so patrons were in the place when I arrived, some drinking and chatting at the bar, others eating a late lunch at tables near the front window. The brick walls and dimly lit green sconces gave the place an east coast feel. Smooth jazz, the kind you'd hear while on hold to speak with a lawyer, played softly.

Caruso sat at a booth on the far side of the bar, near the back. He already had a drink, what looked to be a cola with lime. I ordered a club soda from the bartender and carried it over to the table. The detective was in his mid-forties but looked older. His eyes were sunken and his hair thinning. He'd lost weight since I'd last seem him. His skin had a pallor that didn't seem healthy.

"So what's the deal, Jason? Word is, you quit." He sipped his drink the way you do when there's something harder than soda in the glass. "What's that about?" His voice had a gravelly quality. I remembered him as a smoker. Looking at his physical condition and hearing him speak, a scenario started forming in my head—bad for Caruso, but one that perhaps explained some things.

"Indefinite leave," I said. "After Captain Ellison's death, the job lost some of its meaning for me."

"I never met Ellison, but a few of the guys knew him and said he was a good man."

"One of the best," I said. Captain Germaine Ellison, my boss, had been killed in the line of duty, a victim of the madman responsible for putting Charley in dermatological rehab. My fault on both counts, a guilt that will haunt me the rest of my life.

"Bad break," Caruso said. "As for meaning, going home alive at the end of the day, that's the only one I'm looking for."

"I hear you. Anyway, thanks for agreeing to meet with me."

He nodded and glanced at his watch, then tapped the top of his phone on the table. The screen lit up, but there were no message alerts. "Sorry. I'm waiting on word from my partner about a lead in another case. I'm in a bit of a time crunch. If I gotta go, I'll bolt. Don't take it the wrong way. You know the deal."

"No worries," I said.

He drank some more. "So if you're no longer on the beat, why the interest in the Ryker case?" This time I caught the whiff of rum on his breath.

"Anna is an acquaintance. A friend."

He shook his head. "Terrible thing, huh? I'm guessing she told you she doesn't believe her daughter killed the sister."

"That's right."

"I'm also guessing she wants you to look into things privately."

"Something like that," I said. "I promised her I'd talk to you before even forming an opinion. I also made her promise that, if I felt your case was solid, she'd back down and let you do your job."

"That you're even suggesting there might be something *not* solid is troubling, not to mention insulting."

"The last thing I want to do is second-guess anybody."

"Your way of telling me you come in peace?" He smiled, but there was little humor in his eyes.

"As best as I can."

He shrugged. "A neighbor found the girl wandering the streets at two in the morning. Billie Ryker had blood all over her and carried a knife in her hand that was covered in blood, as well. Both match the victim's type. The size of the knife is consistent with the stab wounds made by the murder weapon. There was more blood in the sink of the bathroom the daughters shared, also matching. The spatter test conducted on Billie's hands was inconclusive because she'd wiped them on her clothes. But still, she was covered in it. Now the kid's supposedly unable to talk." He shrugged. "She's in shock, her mom says."

"What about motive?"

"Sibling stuff. Hatred. Envy."

"You're really hanging your hat on that?" I said.

"Motive in the age of the Internet is different, Jason. The rules have changed. Just look what's happening at schools. Tragic. The teenage mind works differently than ours."

"A prosecutor still needs to be able to point to something specific."

"Several friends said Billie and Janis had had some doozies of public fights in the past few weeks."

This was news to me, something Anna either didn't know about or chose not to share.

"What were the fights about?"

"According to the friends, Billie thought Janis was acting like a slut."

"You're acting like a slut so I think I'll kill you? Come on, Dante."

"No, you come on. Put the badge back on for a moment. If this were your case and you didn't know the family, what would you make of all the evidence I just ran down for you, circumstantial or otherwise?"

"I'm more interested in hearing what you make of it."

"You know what the kid was saying when the officers approached her and the neighbor outside the house? 'I'm sorry. I'm so sorry.' Over and over again. Barely above a whisper. The neighbor, Marty Astor, didn't even seem to notice it, the officer said."

Did Anna know this? Had she refused to accept it? At what point had Billie stopped talking altogether?

"Explain that?" Caruso said. "Sorry for what?"

"Any number of things," I said, though I knew it sounded weak.

He leaned back. "Look, am I a hundred percent good with the call? No. When are we ever? Eighty-five percent, definitely. Ninety percent, maybe. Which, as you know, is usually about as good we can hope for." Caruso finished off the drink. There now was a glaze in his eyes. "I don't want her to be guilty. I don't ever want to believe a thirteen-year-old girl is capable of that kind of violence. Especially not against her own flesh and blood. But my partner and I looked at what was in front of us. And there was a lot to look at. So we made a call. It's what we do. It's how it goes. You know that."

"Where does the DA's office stand?"

"They're behind the arrest."

"Who caught the case?"

"Dick Lipton. He's all over it like Christmas. Slam dunk, he thinks."

Words I didn't want to hear, though they didn't surprise me. Deputy DA Richard Lipton and I had history. None of it good.

"Lipton's an asshole," I said.

"I know how you feel."

"He's also a sloppy prosecutor."

"I swear to you I would love to be wrong. And frankly, I don't care who proves it. If you can, God bless you. But here's your dilemma. A, you're not a cop at the moment. And I somehow doubt you've procured a PI's license since walking away. B, even if you have one, you're asking for a shitstorm from the LAPD if you fuck up our case but don't get better results. Then you're gonna have to go up against Lipton."

"I take it that one is C."

"Nah, it's S for you'd be screwed. He'd probably find a way to arrest you for obstruction." Caruso looked down at his empty glass, maybe debating whether he could afford to have another one.

"There was blood in the bathroom sink, right?" I said.

"Yeah."

"Something's bothering me about that."

"I'm all ears."

"If Billie was wandering the streets with her arms, hands, and clothes covered in blood, and with blood on the knife, as well, who washed off in the bathroom sink?"

Caruso sat back in his chair, the glaze in his eyes clearing. "We figure the blood could've been there for days. Weeks, even."

"The sink had water in it. Right?"

"It could have been there from earlier that night."

I nodded. "Sure. Maybe."

"That's pretty thin, Chance. You know it is."

"Gotta start somewhere."

"Yeah. Just be careful where you end up." His phone buzzed on the tabletop. He scooped it up and studied the screen. "I gotta go." He stood, dropping some tip money on the table. "Between you and me, if you can prove us wrong, I'll buy you a bottle of twelve-year. Just don't mess things up and let a defense lawyer make us all look like morons." He banged his knuckles on the table twice, then turned and ambled out, looking like a man who wanted to be able to move faster than he could.

Driving back to the Valley, I called Anna. "Is Marty still there?"

"Yes. How did it go with Detective Caruso?"

"I'll tell you in a moment. Let me speak with Marty first." I waited while she passed the phone.

"Hello Detective," Marty said.

"To your recollection, did Billie say anything when the cops first arrived?"

"No. She was moaning and wheezing, like she had trouble breathing. I don't remember hearing any specific words. And she sure didn't say anything directly to me. Not from the moment I found her until the police got here."

"Okay." In the background, I heard Anna ask Marty what we were talking about, demanding to know what I was asking him. "One other thing. When you brought Billie back to the house that night, did you get any blood on you?"

"Possibly. I wasn't really paying attention. My focus was on her, and on what had happened."

"Did you by any chance go into the girl's bathroom? Wash your hands, maybe?"

"No."

"You told the police that the front door was open, and that there was blood on the porch and steps."

"Yes."

"A lot of it?"

"Not really. A few drops. Enough to notice."

"Was there more, anywhere else in the house? Other than Janis's bedroom."

"I didn't notice. Sorry. Why?"

I told Marty to put Anna back on.

"He didn't convince you he had a case, did he?" Anna said, coming on the line.

"He's doing everything by the book," I said. "And I don't get the sense he's fumbling things. But I have a few new questions. Can I come by in half an hour?"

Anna had not washed the blood from the sink in Janis and Billie's bathroom, and the few drops of it, now dry and flaking, were still in evidence. The sink basin had long since dried. I took several photos of the drain mouth with my phone, just to have something I could refer to later, if I needed it, as part of my own murder book. I took a series of photos in Janis's bedroom, as well: of the blood-soaked mattress, the spatter pattern on the walls and lamp shade, of the strewn clothes and disarray on her desk.

Returning to the kitchen, I found Anna at the table, staring at an untouched plate of lasagna.

"Marty said goodbye," she told me. "And thank you." She pushed the plate away. "He went to so much trouble, but I just can't eat. I have no appetite."

I sat across from her. "Detective Caruso told me the first-response officers claimed Billie was saying 'I'm sorry,' repeatedly, when they got here."

"Yes, I know. It doesn't mean anything."

"They're looking at it as a confession."

"Well, they're wrong! She was about to go into shock. And I have no proof that's even what she said. Marty never heard it. Even if she did, it could mean anything. I'm sorry I left her alone. I'm sorry I touched her body. I'm sorry my sister is dead!"

"Okay. I agree. Calm down." I put a hand on her arm. I could feel her trembling. "Did Janis have a boyfriend?"

"There was a boy she went out with on occasion. Cameron. A good kid. I liked him."

"Did she see him the night she was killed?"

"No. The police checked. He was out of town with his parents all weekend. They left Friday evening."

"Detective Caruso said Janis's friends told him Billie and she fought recently. In public. That Billie accused Janis of acting like a slut. Caruso's words, not mine."

Anna scowled. "He told me that, as well. It's hard for me to believe it's true. Or if it is, it was a meaningless argument. Kids say stupid things when they're angry. You know that."

"They never fought in front of you?"

"Not over anything of consequence."

I nodded. "Can I have the name and contact number of that friend Janis was supposed to see Saturday night?"

"Of course." Anna crossed to a drawer on the other side

of the kitchen. From it, she took a worn black address book. She thumbed through the pages. "Isabelle Greer. Cell phone is 564-8201. She lives in Woodland Hills."

I inputted the information to my phone. "How well do you know her?"

"Fairly well. She's a sweet girl. Quiet. Moody. With a temper, according to Janis. But they got along well. I'd venture to guess they were best friends."

"The kind of friendship where they'd share personal things?"

"Possibly. They spent a lot of time together." Anna leaned back against the counter. "She might be what you'd call a hostile witness, though. She didn't care much for Billie. Told Janis she was too dark and depressing." Anna seemed to be dismissing as biased or incorrect anything damaging anyone might tell me about Billie and the events of that night. It was a common strategy of defense attorneys: slander the witness, undermine his or her credibility. It was also a tactic of the frightened and desperate.

"I'll keep that in mind," I said.

"What did Detective Caruso say when you told him what I wanted you to do?"

"That nothing would make him happier than for someone to find evidence of another suspect."

"Basically, giving you the go-ahead to do his job."

"Don't look at him as your enemy, Anna. That would be a mistake."

She flared her eyebrows but said nothing.

"If neither Billie nor Marty washed their hands in the sink," I said. "And you didn't touch Janis that night, how'd the blood get there?"

"Seems an obvious question. Why didn't Caruso or his partner ask it?"

"They did, but dismissed it," I said. "They feel the blood could have been left there hours or days, even weeks before."

"Unlikely. Billie is a germaphobe. Her room may be a mess, but she keeps that bathroom spotless."

"It's a thin lead, but it did make me curious."

"Enough to take this on?"

"Yes. I'm going to talk to people in Janis's life, see if I can find out if she was having trouble with anyone. A boyfriend, a jealous rival. Anything that might hint at a threat."

"All things the police should already be doing."

"Let's forget about that for now, okay. I'm going to help you, Anna. As far as I can and as much as I can. I'll share what I find with Detective Caruso. The best scenario would be that I can change his mind and he expands the investigation. That way it's all done properly."

"Do whatever you have to. I understand. And I'll pay you for this. Just tell me how much."

"Nothing. Legally I can't charge you, and I wouldn't if I could."

"Thank you, Jason."

I told her not to thank me yet, that I couldn't make any promises. I didn't tell her that I was afraid of what I might find. Sometimes the most obvious answer is the right one.

7

I called Isabelle Greer as I drove back down Horseshoe Lane. After I identified myself, she asked, "Is this about Janis?"

"I'm a friend of her mother's," I said. "I was hoping I could ask you a few questions."

She paused. "I don't know what I could tell you. I'm still pretty shaken up."

"I understand. I won't take up much of your time."

"Sure, I guess."

"Are you at your home? I'll need to speak with your mother or father first."

"Oh, okay. Hold on." She covered the phone with her hand, muffling her voice as she shouted, "Dad! A friend of Doctor Ryker's needs to talk to you."

The father, a man named Angus, came on the line. "My wife and I are shocked about this," he said. "So tragic. So horrible."

"Would it be all right for me to meet with Isabelle and ask her a few questions? With you or your wife present, of course. I could come to you, or we could connect at a neutral spot. Whatever is most comfortable and convenient."

"Are you a cop? She's already spoken with a detective from the LAPD," he said.

"No, Mr. Greer, I'm working privately for Ms. Ryker," I said.

"Oh, I see. Well, I guess, sure. If it'll help."

We arranged to meet at a Starbucks near their home. I got there first and was halfway through a large cup of coffee when father and daughter walked in. The heavyset Angus had short hair, a chin full of stubble, and the beginnings of a middle-age paunch. Isabelle was flagpole thin, with straight blonde hair that hung down almost to her waist, and a hoop pierced through her nose. After greetings were passed around, Angus said, "I assume Doctor Ryker has asked you to prove Billie didn't kill her, right?"

"Why would you think anyone suspected Billie?" I said. The news of Billie's arrest had not yet been released.

"Miss Ryker told me they busted her," Isabelle said. "When I called the morning after, once I heard what had happened to Janis. And when I spoke with the detectives, they mostly wanted to know about Billie's relationship with Janis. It was obvious who they suspected."

"How did you first hear about her death?" I asked.

"It was all over Twitter," Isabelle said. "I thought it was a joke." She paused, her eyes turning red as she teared up. "I wish it was."

"What were people saying?"

"That somebody butchered her."

"How do you think people found out so quickly?"

"It's the Internet, Mister Chance," Isabelle said. "One neighbor sees the cop cars outside, maybe sees the ambulance take Janis away, asks a question, tells their kid, the kid tweets. It's a cyber epidemic by morning. Then the trolling starts."

"Trolling?"

"Yeah, from creatures that live to cause trouble. Twitter is filled with them. They say stuff just to stir things up. They feed off hatred. And get to stay anonymous."

"What are they saying about Janis?" I asked.

"Stupid things," Isabelle said, "like how she deserved what happened to her. And I bet it's mostly from idiots who didn't even know her. Just assholes who think they're funny and want attention. They post GIFs and memes that make fun of the way she was killed. Like a clip of a victim in one of those Halloween movies, only they replaced the head with Janis's. Really sick, disgusting stuff. Trolls are the pus sores of social media. I wish we could just shut them all down." She'd worked herself up into a minor frenzy. Her father rested a hand on her arm.

"Easy, Issy," he told her. "Calm down." To me, he said, "I'm glad you're investigating this. Somebody needs to get things right. Once again, the Los Angeles Police Department has rushed to judgment. I have a feeling the detectives decided she was guilty because it was the easiest choice for them to make. Easy and lazy." He sounded like Anna. I wondered if they'd spoken after I left her house.

"I'm not in a position to agree or disagree," I said, hoping to avoid a political debate with him about the merits of the LAPD. "Anna Ryker has asked me to look into the case from a new perspective. I don't know what I can prove or disprove. She's worried about her surviving daughter." I turned to Isabelle. "You and Janis were planning on going to the movies that night, correct?"

"We didn't make any specific plans. We'd talked about it

earlier in the day. She said she had some homework to do, so we just decided to see how we felt."

"When did she tell you that she couldn't go?"

"Around 6:30."

"Did she give you a reason?"

"Just that she didn't feel like going."

"Did you get the sense she might have made other plans?"

Isabelle shrugged. She played with strands of her long hair.

"How well do you know Billie?" I asked.

"A little. Just from hanging around with Janis." She frowned and took a deep breath. "She's weird. I mean, I know that sounds callous right now. But I never got a good vibe from her. All that goth stuff, wearing black and red and listening to depressing music. It was freaky. She kind of scared me."

"In what way?"

"I don't know. She just didn't seem normal. Like she was from another planet or something."

"Do you know who told the police they'd witnessed Billie and Janis fighting?" I asked.

"Me," she said. "They asked me if I'd ever seen any kind of conflict between them. I didn't want to lie."

"Tell me about the argument."

"It was after school a couple of weeks ago. We were hanging out in the parking lot. Janis saw Billie off to the side, by herself, and went over to check on her. Then they started yelling at each other. I didn't hear much. At one point, Janis grabbed Billie's arm and Billie pulled away from her. She shouted, 'Keep your hands off me, slut.' Janis looked shocked and hurt. She shoved Billie, and Billie pushed back. Then Billie said, 'You're embarrassing Mom, and you're embarrassing yourself. I fucking hate you.'"

"Embarrassing her how?" I asked.

"I don't know."

"Had you ever seen them argue before?"

"Sure. All the time. Billie was moody and Janis had a temper. A bad combo for sisters."

"Did Janis have a boyfriend?"

"No, not really."

"What about that guy, Cameron?"

"Cam? He and Janis were more like friends. Anyway, he couldn't have done it. I called him right after I heard. He was in Vegas with his parents all weekend."

"Any other guys she dated, or was friends with?"

"Not that she ever told me about." Her fingers tapped nervously on the tabletop. "She said the boys in class were mostly morons. She felt she was way above them."

"She preferred older guys?"

She nodded quickly, then seemed to catch herself, and said, "I guess. Maybe."

Sensing she was holding back, I said, "Anna mentioned she thought Janis had been seeing an older guy." It was a lie, Anna had said no such thing, but I hoped the comment might prod Isabelle into letting go. When she blushed, I added, "Someone in college." She sank back in her seat, twisting her lips to the side, looking troubled. "You might as well tell me who he is," I said, gambling. "I'll find out, anyway. It will just take me longer and slow down my investigation."

"You think I know?"

"I think maybe you're embarrassed. Which is probably why you kept it from the police. But I'm not the cops. And

The Bad Side of Good 53

there's no judgment here. Not toward you or Janis. I'm just trying to get at the truth."

She scratched the bottom of her nose with the top of her index finger. Her eyes were tearing up again.

"Whatever you know, Issy, you have to tell Mister Chance," her father said. "Now is not the time to hold anything back."

"Okay. Fine. She talked about this guy named Paige. Older. In college, like you said."

"What's the last name?" I asked.

"I don't want to get anybody in any trouble. Janis boasted about a lot of things that weren't true."

"You need to tell me Paige's last name if you know it."

"Okay, but you never heard this from me. Paige Leary. His dad is some big TV producer. You know that Netflix sci-fi series, *Outer Rim*? That's his show."

"Janis claimed she was dating Paige?"

"That they'd gone out a few times. Like I said, who knows if it was true. I never met him."

"Did she act like it was serious?"

"What's serious when you're sixteen? She said he was hot."

"Were they sleeping together?"

Isabelle paused before saying, "Yeah. She told me he was her first."

"I'm sorry," Angus said. "This convo's getting a little uncomfortable for me. I guess I'm edgy about the whole thing."

"Dad, don't be a prude," Isabelle said. "Teens have sex. Get over it."

"I'm in the same boat, Mr. Greer. My daughter Kathy is seventeen."

"Janis liked Kathy," Isabelle said, as though relieved to

be able to change the subject. "She thought your daughter was cool."

"That's comforting to hear. Do you think Billie knew about Paige? Could that be what she meant when she called Janis a slut?"

"I doubt it," Isabelle said. "Janis never told Billie or her mom anything."

"But she often confided things to you."

"We were best friends."

"Did she tell you how she met Paige?"

"Yeah," Isabelle said. "That's another thing that never made sense and made me doubt it was true. She said he was a patient of her mom's. I mean, that's a giveaway right there that she was lying, right? Who dates a guy your *shrink* mom is treating?"

I CALLED CARUSO AND FILLED HIM IN.

"Funny, his name never came up when we interviewed Isabelle," Caruso said.

"Because you were focused on Billie. I had to pry it out of her. She said she didn't want to get anyone in trouble. She was scared to bring it up. And I get the feeling she thinks Billie's guilty."

"I wonder why," Caruso said, then was overcome by a fit of coughing. "Sorry. Damn summer colds."

"Everything okay, Dante?"

He paused. His silence spoke volumes.

"How bad?" I asked.

"You could tell right off, couldn't you?"

"I had a feeling."

"Lung cancer," he said. "Stage four."

"Jesus. I'm sorry."

"Three packs a day for twenty-five stress-filled years had to come with a price, didn't it?"

"Why are you still working? You should be focusing on beating the damned thing."

He laughed, sadly. "You don't beat stage four, compadre. And hell, I always figured I'd die on the job. Why change now? For the record, it's not making me sloppy. I'd have arrested the girl if I were the healthiest man walking the street."

Perhaps he was telling the truth.

According to information I gathered online, Paige was a product of television producer Adam Leary's second marriage to a film actress named Michelle LeBron. Adam and Michelle divorced a few years after a younger brother, Wyatt, was born. Wyatt was seventeen, Paige twenty. Adam never remarried and lived a very public bachelor life. He'd recently come under fire: allegations of sexual misconduct from several members of his staff. Given the wave of abuse scandals sweeping through Hollywood, most in the industry expected him to either be asked by the network to step down from the show, or to be fired.

His oldest son Paige attended the University of Southern California as a sophomore in their coveted film department, studying to be a director. He'd been arrested twice on DUI charges and had gone to a rehab center in Malibu after each arrest. He never stayed longer than a month—the minimum treatment time at the center. I had a suspicion his therapy sessions with Anna Ryker were either court-mandated or something his father or mother demanded he go through along with the rehab, possibly under threat of withholding whatever allowance they were giving him if he refused.

Paige had his own website, one that mainly consisted of blogs about living rich and single in LA, with photos of the young man tooling around town: selfies taken at clubs, concerts, or simply while driving his BMW convertible down the Strip or along Pacific Coast Highway. In the pictures, he looked older than his twenty years—which is probably what allowed him access to the clubs. That and the fact that he knew the right people.

There was a link on his site to a YouTube video of a short film he'd made as a freshman at USC. It was called *Don't Turn Out the Lights*: ten minutes of a teenage girl, alone in a house, stalked by some unseen intruder. The film was shot from the POV of the stalker, using moody lighting and amateurish handheld camera moves to show how the villain spied on the girl and followed her around the empty house. Paige used every slasher movie cliché he could think of: a phone ringing with no one on the other end of the call; light bulbs flickering then going out; a cat jumping from a closet as the frightened girl slowly opened the door after hearing a noise; a gloved hand reaching into frame and taking a knife from a rack in the kitchen followed by the intruder's shadow moving across the wall.

At the climax of the film, the intruder chased the girl into her bedroom and pinned her down on the mattress. Then—in what I'm sure Paige thought was a clever twist—the girl pulled another knife from under her pillow and jammed it into the intruder's chest. Then she flipped him over so she was on top. The perspective changed at that point, from the intruder's POV to hers, as she stabbed her stalker to death. Fake blood splattered liberally—on her, on the sheets, on the walls—as she arced the knife up and down. This was caught by a second camera, the footage intercut with her POV angle, and all of it shown in slow motion.

I found the film amateurish and sloppy. Paige didn't seem to have much original talent. But the similarities to Janis's murder were striking—and too strong to ignore.

8

I heard a knock on the study door, then Charley said, "Can I come in?"

"Please do." I closed the lid on the laptop.

She was dressed for bed in sweats and a pressure garment pajama top. The compression was intended to combat scarring and ease some of the lingering pain. Tight-fitting, it molded to her athletic body like exercise wear.

"If you tell me I look sexy," she said, "I swear I'll nut-kick you."

I put my hands up, defensively.

"I can't sleep," she said. "I was going to get some tea and saw the light under the door. Want a cup?"

We brewed chamomile in the kitchen then we went onto the back deck. Dawn was still a few hours away, and the air was cool. A thin mist made the backyard lamps glow. In the light, I looked at the patched fissure in the back wall—a dark smear across the cinderblocks—and the broken trellis and bougainvillea branches on the ground below it. I'd uncharacteristically left the job half-done, all because of one phone call.

I told Charley about my afternoon.

"I knew you wouldn't be able to stay out of it," Charley said.

I mimicked Pacino's line from *Godfather III*. "Just when I think I'm out…"

"Don't blame them for pulling you back in," she said. "You had a choice."

I nodded, leaning forward and placing my folded arms across my thighs. My neck and head ached from too much time at the computer. "I think someone else was in the house that night, besides Billie and Janis," I said. "Somebody else washed blood off in the girl's sink. Maybe they came in after Billie ran out with the knife. A random thief who saw the front door open and decided to snoop around and see what they could pilfer. Could be they found the body, touched it, or touched something else with Janis's blood on it." I paused. "Or it was done by the killer."

"How do you know that blood came from the night of the murder?" Charley said.

"Caruso said the same thing. His excuse for not pursuing it. And I don't know it did."

"You don't know, yet you do."

"Something like that." I told her about Paige Leary. "I'm hoping I can persuade Anna to let me see the recordings of her sessions with him."

"Recordings?"

"Part of her practice is to video her one-on-ones, so she doesn't have to take notes while they're talking. It allows her more direct contact with the patient. She's been doing it for years. Since she started out."

"Do you really think you'll pick up something by watching them that a trained psychiatrist didn't notice the first go-round?"

"I'm hoping she'll agree to view them with me. Look at them from a new perspective."

"Sounds like you'd be putting her on the spot."

"I know. And that's the part that bothers me. But her oldest daughter is dead, and her other one is facing a murder charge. You'd think that might outweigh her professional ethics."

"It still would be asking a lot of her."

"She came to me."

"True." Charley sipped tea. "I'm glad she did. I wanted you to make the choice to help her. You're too good at what you do to not be doing it."

"That's high praise, coming from you."

She laughed. "Right. The Wonder Kid. I'm so great at it, I almost got myself burned to death."

"Stop."

"Anyway, we're not talking about me." She took hold of my hand. "And I'm glad you've got something to focus on *other* than worrying about me."

"I'll never stop worrying about you." I leaned in to give her a kiss on the lips. She tensed, pulling back to avoid it and turning her head.

"Not yet," she said.

I didn't insist, just put my arms around her and held her close. Soon, she was asleep on my shoulder. I didn't move for fear of waking her. I would've stayed like that the rest of the night, as long as she was comfortable and close to me. Anna Ryker had other plans.

I answered her call after a single ring, whispering a greeting.

"Someone's been in the house," Anna said.

"A burglar?"

"I'm not sure. I don't think anything is missing. But someone definitely broke in."

"Have you called the police?"

"Not yet."

"Do that now. Is Billie all right?"

"She's sleeping."

I glanced down at Charley, conflicted. Finally, I said, "I'll be right over."

THE SUN WAS JUST CRESTING THE RIM OF THE SAN GABRIEL Mountains behind me as I exited the 101 onto Topanga Canyon. Pink and orange clouds glowed in my rearview mirror, a dazzling view of which I never tire. The morning commute out of the canyon had begun, cars moving slowly in both directions, and it took me twenty minutes to reach Anna's house. A beige Crown Victoria sedan sat next to Anna's Volvo—occupying my usual spot—and I had to drive to the top of the hill and park in the cul-de-sac.

Reporters and cameramen stood beside local news vans across the narrow stretch of road from Anna's property. One approached me as I walked back down the hill, calling out my name as I started up Anna's steps. He knew I'd taken a leave of absence from the sheriff's department and wanted to know what part I played in the investigation. *Was I working privately for the family?*

"No comment," I said, waving a hand, hurrying up the stairs and into the house.

Caruso sat at the kitchen table with a mug of coffee in his hand, looking disgruntled. Anna stood by the sink. Her appearance had further deteriorated, marred by fear, exhaustion, personal neglect.

"Morning," I said.

Caruso grunted, nodding once. "I gotta tell you, you're not making my life any easier."

"Unless you think I'm the one who broke in," I said, "I'm not sure what you mean."

He smirked. "Me, either, actually. I'm just being surly. I need to bitch at somebody." He took a sip of his coffee, glancing over at Anna. "This is good, thanks."

She wasn't paying attention to him. She stared down at a cell phone as it lit up in her hand with an incoming call. "How'd the press get my number?" she asked. "They're calling nonstop, leaving messages, requesting an interview."

"They pay to get the number," I said. "There are plenty of people willing to sell, too. Usually employees of a carrier, looking to make some extra cash and hoping they don't get caught."

"I wish I could keep the press away from you," Caruso said. "Unfortunately, the First Amendment protects even scumbags who pretend to be journalists."

"I saw the vans outside," I said. "Did any more of the story get out?"

"They know about Billie now," Anna said.

"Shit," I said, glancing at Caruso.

He raised a defensive hand. "We didn't leak it, compadre. Nobody thought we could contain it forever, did they?"

"How is Billie?" I asked Anna.

"No change, physically or emotionally," she said.

Caruso stood and set his coffee cup on the counter beside the sink, stepping past me as he did. Up close, I could see the redness of exhaustion in his eyes. He hadn't shaved, and the stubble on his chin and jaw was almost completely gray. He smelled of coffee and sweat. Something else, as well, a darker scent underneath, not easily recognizable. But one I knew.

"So," he said to Anna, "about the break-in ..."

"Come on," she said. "I'll show you."

We followed her through the living room to a short corridor on its other side. A door at the end opened to the office anteroom: a small enclosure with a rustic bench against one wall and a large purple and green dreamcatcher hanging above it. New Age magazines were arranged across a coffee table. There was a reception desk to the right of a second door that opened into Anna's office.

"Someone was in here last night," Anna said, stepping over to the desk. On it, a laptop computer sat open, surrounded by neatly stacked envelopes, notepads, and a rectangular calendar of five-by-seven pages on a spiral loop.

"What makes you think so?" Caruso asked.

"Jillian, my office assistant, never leaves the laptop open when she leaves for the night, per my request."

"Maybe she forgot," he said.

"She's been with me almost a year and never has, not once. She's very thorough. Also, the calendar is facing the opposite direction, away from the desk chair. See?" Anna was right; the page for the current month had been turned away from whomever might sit at the desk, toward the door. "I'm thinking someone knocked it over then righted it," Anna said. "In their haste, they placed it the wrong way."

Caruso picked up the booklet, looked at it, then put it back on the desk, facing the correct direction. He appeared unimpressed. "What else?"

She led us into her main office and session room. The sky outside the picture windows was brightening as the sun rose over the treetops of the canyon, flooding the room with light. Despite this, the office felt cold and stuffy.

Anna pointed to an open curtain on a pressure rod fixed between the two sides of a jamb that framed a kitchenette. "I pulled that closed over the kitchen area the last time I was in here," she said. "I've not come back in since, not until this morning. Yet the curtain is open."

"That's all?" Caruso said. He was losing patience.

"No. Over here, look at this." She stepped to a cabinet and pulled open the bottom drawer, where she kept the tapes of her sessions. "My tapes are out of order."

"Tapes?" Caruso said.

"I record my sessions with a mini-DV camera." She gestured to a small camcorder on a tripod by the window. "I store them chronologically. I'm a stickler about it. Three of them were removed, then put back in, but in the wrong spot."

Caruso stooped down to get a better look at the rows of clear plastic containers with white interior jackets and neat, handwritten dates on their spines. I looked over his shoulder. August 8th, 15th, and 22nd were sandwiched in between August 7th and 9th. A mistake probably done in haste, maybe with only the light from a flashlight or smartphone screen as guidance. If, indeed, there had been a robbery.

"A common mistake," Caruso said. "Done in haste when you last looked at them."

"I don't make those kinds of mistakes," Anna said. I heard pride as well as defiance in her voice.

"Do those dates have any significance to you?" I asked.

"Not off the top of my head," Anna said. "I'd need to check my notes."

"Yeah, why don't you do that?" Caruso said.

"One other thing." She stepped past us, to a small bookshelf that held several hardback psychiatric tomes on one shelf, some framed photographs on another, and a collection of small clay figures that looked crude and childish on a third. The statues were of animals, all disproportionately sculpted and sloppily painted. "Janis and Billie made these one year when they went together to camp," Anna said. "They were eight and five at the time."

I had similar creations in the living room of our home, made by Kathy in an arts and crafts tent at a street fair I'd taken her to when she was young. Janis's and Billie's animals came in pairs—two horses, two sheep, two turtles, two frogs—except one: a solitary bird with its wings spread.

"The second bird is missing," I said.

Anna nodded.

"Whose? Janis's or Billie's?"

Anna lifted the bird and showed me the bottom. Billie's name had been scratched into the clay before it dried, meaning Janis's creation was the one missing.

"You sure you didn't just misplace the other?" Caruso said.

"I haven't touched them in years. They've stayed right here."

"How about your assistant. Or a housecleaner?"

"Jillian wouldn't mess with them," Anna said. "And I don't have a housekeeper."

"Maybe a patient lifted it at some point?" I offered.

"It's possible," Anna said. "But why?"

"Why does anybody do anything?" Caruso said. He didn't seem to be buying any of this.

"You haven't been in here since Janis was killed?" I asked.

"I've canceled my sessions for the entire week."

"Understandable," I said, knowing Kathy was one of those cancellations.

"So why'd you decide to come in this morning?" Caruso asked.

"I was looking for a book on grief." She reached for a

volume on the shelf, *A Grief Observed*, by C.S. Lewis. "I noticed the computer and the calendar out in the reception area and immediately knew something was off. Once I came into the office and saw the open curtain, I forgot about the book and did a search, starting with my video files. That's when I called you, Jason."

"The missing bird statue is curious, sure," Caruso said. "If it's actually missing and not just misplaced." He paused before adding, "I'd like to have a team come in and look around the office again, if that's all right with you, Ms. Ryker."

"Of course," she said.

"You're welcome to stay," Caruso told me. "As long as you keep out of the team's way."

I decided it would be best if I didn't hang around. I didn't want this to turn into a battle of egos, even if Caruso was starting to act like maybe he thought it was. I preferred he be the one to find the evidence that proved Billie's innocence. "I've got some things I need to deal with, but thanks. Anna, could I speak with you a moment?"

We left Caruso and stepped outside, onto the porch that ran the length of the house and office. The sun was high above the canyon now. The day had begun to heat up.

"It's a good sign, no?" she said. "That he wants to bring the team back."

"Yes."

"Is it odd he returned?" It took me a moment to realize she didn't mean Caruso; she was referring to the killer.

"Maybe," I answered. "Maybe not. Until we know the identity, we shouldn't jump to conclusions." She looked frustrated, hearing this. "I need to ask you about a patient of yours. Paige Leary."

"Paige? What does he have to do with anything?"

"Isabelle told me Janis and he had been seeing each other."

"That's highly unlikely," she said. "I don't think they ever met. Isabelle must be mistaken."

"Why were you treating him?"

"I can't answer that."

I'd expected this response. "Have you seen the short film he made at USC?" Anna shook her head. "It's pretty gruesome. And it set off some alarms when I watched it. I'd like to pursue."

She tensed. "How?"

"I'd like to look at your session files. Only Paige's tapes."

"You know what my answer is going to be, Jason."

"I'm hoping you'll surprise me. We could view them together."

Anna leaned back against the porch railing. This for her was the professional equivalent of a holdup at gunpoint, the thief demanding his victim hand over something personal and sacred, like a wedding ring.

"Paige hasn't been in for several months," she said, at last. "His final session with me was in—" she stopped, her eyes widening as she made the connection. "Oh Lord. It was August. August 22nd, I think."

The last date of the three misplaced tapes, each a week apart.

9

Caruso caught up with me at my car. "You see what she's trying to do, right?" he said, wheezing and trying to catch his breath. The climb down Anna's steps, followed by the ascent up the road to the cul-de-sac, had winded him. "I mean, come on. A closed computer? An about-face calendar on a desk? Three mini-DV tapes in the wrong place in a cabinet? And the pièce de résistance, that missing clay figure. She's working a little too hard, you ask me."

I couldn't fault him for his suspicions; her evidence of a break-in was simplistic and easily staged. Anna could have set the whole thing up, hoping to create doubt in Caruso's mind so he'd turn his focus away from Billie. But I didn't think she had done that. Caruso didn't know her like I did. If she honestly thought her daughter might be guilty, or if she were to learn something that proved Billie's culpability beyond a shadow of a doubt, Anna would face the music.

At least I wanted to believe so.

"Let's wait for whatever your team uncovers," I said.

"I wouldn't hold my breath. By the way, the DA's sending

in a psychiatrist to evaluate Billie tomorrow. Maybe he or she can get through to the kid. This whole thing would be a lot easier if she could answer some questions."

"Does Anna know?"

"Yeah, I told her. She wasn't happy. But what can she do? It's not her call."

"Maybe you'll get lucky."

"What are you planning?"

"I want to meet with Paige Leary, if you've no problem with that."

"Knock yourself out. After the stunt Anna Ryker just pulled, I still believe Billie's our best bet. Anna knows it, too, and she's scared. That's what this is all about. Just let me know what Paige has to say, if anything."

"Of course," I said.

He lumbered back down the hill to his car. A reporter jumped in his path. I heard the woman ask, "Detective Caruso, does the DA have enough evidence to take Billie Ryker to trial?"

"Get out of my face," Caruso said and climbed into his sedan.

ANNA HAD RELUCTANTLY GIVEN ME A CONTACT NUMBER FOR Paige. Once I was out of the canyon, I called it. I was told by an electronic message that the number had been deactivated. Next, I contacted the University of Southern California, lied that I was still a sheriff's detective—even gave my old badge number—and said I urgently needed to contact Paige Leary in connection with an ongoing murder investigation. Normally, I would have needed a warrant, but the USC staff didn't seem aware of that fact, or did not care, and after being patched through to various departments, I eventually obtained a new cell phone number for the young man.

"This is Paige," a voice said on the message greeting. "I'm in class, or shooting something cool, or I'm in the editing room hating what I just shot. Leave a message and I'll call you back as soon as I come up for air."

After the tone, I said, "Paige, my name is Jason Chance. I'm an acquaintance of Doctor Anna Ryker. I'm sure you've heard by now about her daughter, Janis. I would like to speak with you if you don't mind. I'm not a cop or a reporter, just a friend with a couple of questions. I do think we should speak."

Charley and Kathy were in the kitchen fixing a late breakfast of fruit and yogurt when I got home. I speared a slice of pineapple with a fork from a big plate in the center of the table and munched on it, watching a fly crawl across the pane of the sink window. My heel bounced up and down like Adam Clayton pounding his bass drum during U2's "Vertigo."

Charley noticed this; she stared at me across the rim of her tea mug. "You okay?"

I nodded.

"Kathy had another dream," Charley said. "This one is more obscure and disturbing."

"Tell me all about it," I said.

"Why?" Kathy said. "So you can tell me again it's just my subconscious and has nothing to do with the case?"

"I reserve that right, yes," I said. "But I'll keep an open mind going in."

"Swear."

I held up three fingers.

"Okay. We were in some forest. Janis and me."

"Janis and I," I said, correcting her.

"See? There you go!"

"Sorry. Please, continue."

"Janis and *I* were in some forest, and she was leading me by the hand. It looked like one of those horror-movie locations. You know, huge trees with crooked branches and big roots coming out of the ground, the kind that look like serpent's tails."

"Delightful imagery," I said.

"Shush," Charley said.

"I know it sounds a little cheesy as I recount it," Kathy said. "But the place was scary as hell while I dreamed it."

"I'm sure," I said.

"I knew in the dream that it was an evil place. A dangerous one. And I didn't want to be there. I kept telling Janis we had to turn back, that we were going the wrong way. She wouldn't listen. And her grip on my hand was so strong, I couldn't pull away. She said, 'You have to see this.' I finally just gave up and let her lead me deeper into the woods. It was getting dark, and there were weird sounds all around. Cats meowing and babies crying, all mixed together. And oddly, phones ringing. But not normal rings. Music ringtones."

"Did you recognize them?" I asked.

"I did in the dream. One of them, anyway. A song by that old band you like. The Cure. I knew the lyrics and everything, just from hearing the melody. Which is weird because in life I'd never heard it and I don't like the band."

"Your loss," I said. "What was the song?"

"Something about a little black-haired girl."

"'One Hundred Years,'" I said. "From the *Pornography* album."

"Really?" Kathy said. "That's all you needed to know to guess it?"

"He's the rock and roll king, remember?" Charley said.

"I wonder if it's some reference to Billie," Kathy said. "Because of the black hair."

"Probably," I said, trying to sound like I was buying into this.

"So we came to this clearing, but it was just as dark there as it had been in the forest. Maybe even darker. In the center of the small field, there was a house. Southern looking, like New Orleans. What are they called? With the big balconies on the second floor?"

"Antebellum," Charley said.

"Yeah, that's it. White, with black shutters, and a wrought iron railing on the lower and upper porches. One of those dreamcatchers hung by the front door, like the one in Doctor Ryker's waiting room. This one wasn't green and purple, though; it was all white with a little red. The red on it looked like bloodstains. Seeing the house, Janis pointed to a window, where I saw the silhouette of a man."

"Did you recognize him?" I asked.

Kathy shook her head. "He was just a shadow. Janis dropped to her knees, screaming and putting her hands over her ears. Then she said this weird thing. 'The Sins of the Father have ruined the music.'"

"Weird, for sure," I said. "What happened next?"

"I woke up."

"How many dreams is this, now?" Charley asked.

"Just the two," Kathy said. "And I don't think it's coincidence or my subconscious at work, like you suggested, Dad. I think the dreams are coming from Janis, and that she's trying to give me answers."

"I agree," Charley said.

"The dreamcatcher," Kathy said. "That scary house. The

music. Last time it was Zeppelin and the Stones. Now the Cure. What was the song? 'A Thousand Years'?"

"'One Hundred Years,'" I said.

"Maybe that's what it feels like to Janis," Kathy said. "Being a ghost. Trapped in a netherworld. Like that movie with Casey Affleck. *A Ghost Story*. Could be she doesn't even know who killed her. She just has pieces of evidence that she's trying to give to you. Through me."

"I think we're getting a little carried away here," I said.

"There are more things in your heaven and earth, Horatio ..." Charley said.

"Yeah, but most of them you can't take into court," I said.

"There you go again," Kathy said. "Why do I bother? I *know* it's true. Janis is speaking to me. And we need to listen." She got up and left the room.

Charley frowned. "Well played, Mr. Skeptic." She picked up her tea mug and followed Kathy out.

My cell rang. The screen read: UNKNOWN CALLER. I answered, identifying myself.

A male voice said, "This is Paige Leary. You wanted to talk to me?"

HE LOOKED MORE LIKE AN ACTOR THAN A STUDENT DIRECTOR: blonde, of medium height, muscular, his eyes a deep blue color, his face suntanned. Long, shaggy brown hair kept falling down across his forehead as he spoke, and he constantly and aggressively shoved it back with his fingers. He wore white chino cut-offs shredded at the knees, red and white high-top basketball shoes, and a T-shirt for a Francis Coppola film called *Rumblefish*.

We met at a small vegan restaurant on Gower, in Hollywood, where a waiter gave us hand-printed menus and put down empty glasses for a bottle of water already set on the table, sealed with an old-fashioned rubber stopper.

"I appreciate your meeting me," I said.

"I'm curious, for sure," he said. "How do I fit into this?"

"What do you know about Janis's murder?"

"Just what I read in the paper. Pretty messed up, huh? The mom must be sick about it."

"She's distraught, yes."

"And the younger one is in a coma, right?" He pulled the stopper on the water bottle and filled both our glasses. "I guess when you kill your sister, it can freak you out." He waited for me to respond. I said nothing. He took a drink of water. "I read when they found her she was covered in Jan's blood and holding the murder weapon."

"Evidence is a funny thing."

"You sound like a cop."

"Sheriff's homicide, but I'm on a leave of absence."

"What happened? The job got to be too much?"

"Something like that."

"So this is a private investigation?"

"Doctor Ryker and I are friends. I told her I'd do some snooping around."

"And that brought you to me. Why?"

"How well did you know Janis?"

"I met her once. Through Doctor Ryker. She was my therapist. Part of a DUI sentencing. I only had to go for six weeks, but I liked it and kept it up. I appreciated her style. Yoga, meditation. And as a writer/director, it's good to have a clear path to your psyche."

"Your last session was back in August. Why'd you stop?"

"School began. I got busy. It was hard to juggle everything. I thought we were talking about Janis."

"Yes, and how you met her."

"I was leaving a session and she was coming home from school. I said hello. She told me her name. That was about it."

"I heard you two had dated."

"Nope. Who said that?"

"A friend of hers."

"One of her little girlfriends?" He scoffed. "I met Jan the one time. That's it." He looked over at a couple of mid-twenties women just taking their seats at a corner table. When one of them glanced at him, he smiled and winked. They blushed and giggled. Paige Leary definitely was a player.

The waiter returned. Paige ordered a tempeh burger with a side of sweet potato fries. I said I'd just have coffee. The waiter began to recite a list of organic brews available, but I stopped him after he'd mentioned three. "You pick," I said.

He scampered away.

"My dad did a cop show a few years back," Paige said. "A guy from Sheriff's consulted. Pepper or Feiffer, something like that."

"Harry Feiffer?"

"I think so. You know him?"

"Our paths have crossed."

"Six degrees, huh."

"Speaking of degrees, you never met Billie?" I asked.

"Nope. So crazy, isn't it? Thirteen years old. You never know about anybody."

I paused, then said, "I watched your student film."

"Oh, okay. Now I get why you're here. That stupid movie." He drank some water, too quickly, and a little dribbled down his chin. "I was a freshman, man, learning my craft. Mood and camera angles. That's what I was after." He wiped away the water with the back of his hand. "I didn't have time for a story, so I used every cliché I could think of from every slasher movie I'd ever seen."

"Still, the similarities are curious."

"Come on, I'd be the biggest moron in town to kill someone the same way as in a movie I made. This isn't *Basic Instinct*. I'd be smarter than that."

"Where were you Saturday night?"

He laughed. "Jesus, you *do* suspect me. I was with a friend, helping edit a music video."

"Your place? His place? The school editing bays?"

"He's a she. And we were at her place. Until very late."

"What do you consider late?" Though I assumed whomever he'd been with would give him whatever alibi he asked of them.

"You know, I'm flattered," Paige said. "Really. It's cool how you're trying to make me out to be some psycho. Are you going to try and trick me into confessing? Are you wearing a wire? Are some cops waiting in a van out in the alley?"

"None of the above. I'm just asking questions."

He attempted a Joe Friday voice. "I'm just asking questions." This made him chuckle. "I guess a lot of cops become PIs, huh. Do you have a license? Do you need one?" He spoke with a manic energy, as if some drug had just kicked in.

The waiter brought my coffee. It was too hot and too strong to drink. I poured in some milk to cool it off.

"Who pointed you in my direction?" Paige said. "Anna?"

"Why do you ask?"

"It's interesting if she did," Paige said. "Maybe she had a reason. To create doubt about Billie's guilt. She is a psychiatrist, smart enough to think up some clever mind-fuck like that, don't you think?"

"Smart enough? Absolutely. Would she do it? Not in a million years."

"What's that line from *Chinatown*? At the right time and place, we're all capable of anything."

The waiter brought Paige his food: a vegan patty on a gluten-free bun and a stack of orange-colored fries in a cone of beige paper. It all smelled heavily condiment-filled. He slathered the top piece of the bun with organic mustard.

"You're way off base," he said. "I've got no motive. I didn't know the girl, despite what her chirpies may have told you, and all the evidence points to the sister. If the LAPD buys that, why can't you?" He bit into his burger and chewed, speaking as he did. "It's a great idea for a movie, though. Psychiatrist frames a patient to protect her guilty daughter/lover/husband. Thanks, Detective. This lunch wasn't a waste of time, after all."

I walked out of the restaurant thinking he had all the confidence and arrogance he'd need to succeed as a director, and wondering why he kept referring to Janis, a girl he claimed he'd met only once, as *Jan*, when not even her mother did.

ADAM LEARY WAS DISTURBINGLY TALL; WHEN WE SHOOK hands, he had to stoop forward because of the height difference. He was middle-aged, lean and well-built from gym work, swimming, or tennis. Despite this, he was not what you would call a classically attractive man. He had sunken cheeks, a lazy eye, and skin marred by sun wrinkles and moles he probably should have checked out by a dermatologist. We met on the Paramount lot, at a suite of offices inside what looked like a trailer, after a call from him requesting the meeting.

"Have a seat," he said, his voice deep and oracular as he motioned to one of two chairs on the visitor's side of his desk. "Thanks for coming here. I appreciate it. I've got a busy day. Leaving the studio would have shot it all to hell."

"Well, you did call me, Mr. Leary. Plus, it's always fun for me to visit the studios. I love old Hollywood."

Despite the trailer shell, the office suite had been done up to replicate the older offices of the main buildings. The walls were paneled, the furniture heavy, the dark Venetian blinds slanted so they let only thin shafts of sunlight into the room. Framed posters hung on the walls: Hitchcock's *Vertigo*, Ridley Scott's *Blade Runner*, William Friedkin's *The Exorcist,* Polanski's *Chinatown*. *Like father, like son,* I thought, looking at this last one. Nothing in the office referenced any of Leary's television shows. Over the years, I've met a lot of TV people who privately disdain the medium of their success. *Born for the movies*, they'd say. *Settled for television*.

"I understand you spoke with my son," Leary said.

"Less than an hour ago, yes. He must have called you before he finished his tempeh burger."

"No, I called him. I knew he was meeting with you. I was curious how it went. And why you thought to question him in regard to a murder about which he knows nothing."

"I simply wanted to verify that fact," I said.

"Are you a parent, Mr. Chance?"

"I am. A daughter. Almost 18."

"That's a tough age. Especially with girls, I imagine. I have two boys."

"I know."

"As a father, you can understand a parent's sense of protectiveness. When someone starts asking his son questions relating to a murder investigation, well ..." He leaned back in his massive chair. "Want to know what's most disturbing? Paige said you're not even with the police."

"I'm on leave from the sheriff's department."

"What did you do to get suspended?"

"I wasn't. It was my choice."

"Oh, I see." He crossed his arms. "So now you're, what? A private investigator? *'Forget it, Jake, it's Chinatown.'*" He nodded toward the poster on the wall. "Greatest PI movie of all time."

I didn't dispel him of the notion I was a *shamus*, as he would have probably called me if I let him keep rambling. He was a man who talked like the movies he seemed to love. Though I suspected the rambling was intentional. He was sizing me up. Checking to see how much of a threat I posed. It was why he'd wanted to meet in person. And why he'd summoned me to his turf.

"How familiar are you with the Janis Ryker murder investigation?" I asked.

"Only the stuff I've read. Horrible thing. She was what, sixteen?"

"That's right."

"And her thirteen-year-old sister killed her."

"She's the prime suspect. Anna Ryker has asked me to do some research on my own."

"I'm sure the LAPD is thrilled."

"I know the investigating detective. We've reached an understanding."

"And somebody told you Paige and Janis dated. My son says it isn't true."

"Yes, he told me. I've received contradictory statements."

"Must put you in a pickle. What's a shamus to do?" I suppressed a smile. He'd found a way to sneak in the term. "I believe my son."

"I don't believe or disbelieve him," I said. "I'm simply asking questions."

He turned and looked toward the slats of the window blinds. "I've done a few cop shows. Worked with a guy from Sheriff's on one. Harry Feiffer. You know him?"

"Yes."

"Nice guy. Good cop. Very helpful. The show was praised for its verisimilitude. Probably why it bombed. People don't want real in their entertainment. They want life with all the boring parts taken out." He pointed to the poster for *Vertigo*. "Hitchcock said that."

"What about your other son, Wyatt?" I said. "Did he ever mention meeting Janis or Billie?"

"Not that I recall. I don't much keep up with my children's social life. I don't want to be that kind of dad. The one who needs to *know everything*." He made air quotes with his fingers as he said this. "I trust my boys."

This from a man who a moment ago talked about a father's protectiveness. I had a feeling the latter statement was a better insight than the former into Adam Leary's paternal instincts, and that any protectiveness grew out of fear that his sons might have done, or would do, something that could adversely affect his own sexual misconduct investigation.

A cell phone on his desk lit up. He leaned forward to read whatever message had come in. Behind him, the iMac on his credenza *beeped* continually with incoming email messages.

"When was the last time you talked with Wyatt?" I asked.

"I haven't seen him in days. I got a text last Friday night, telling me he was going to spend the weekend in Laguna with some friends."

"Do you know who these friends are? I'd like to speak with Wyatt if I could."

"Look, Mister Chance, I understand why Doctor Ryker asked you to look into things. She's hoping you'll prove her daughter's innocence. She's a concerned mother. More power to her." He leaned forward, placing his hands on the desktop. Even seated, he loomed over me. "But neither of my boys had anything to do with the tragic murder of that girl. To even consider otherwise is ludicrous. I shall warn you once. Stay away from Paige. Stay away from Wyatt. Stay away from me. Or I'll have my lawyer so far up your ass, you'll think he's a case of diarrhea. Now, I'm a busy man; please see yourself out."

It was a melodramatic dismissal. The diarrhea comment was probably a line from one of his TV shows.

"Thank you for your time, Mister Leary."

Outside the trailer, in a small park-like courtyard, a young woman in a blue coat and black skirt led tourists on a studio tour. Closer to me, two actors in Fifties wardrobe and full makeup sat on a bench, smoking. The walkways between the office buildings and sound stages were wide, crowded with people moving quickly from one location to another, some with scripts in their hands, others with cups of coffee and open iPads, off which they read emails and texts as they moved. The hustle and bustle of the world of illusion. A world filled with braggadocios like Leary, their broad demeanor and boastful arrogance masking a dark heart capable of sexual harassment, abuse—and sometimes things even more sinister.

A STRONG WIND CAME ON AS I DROVE BACK TO THE VALLEY, the traffic light swaying like a ringing bell while I waited at the intersection of Mulholland and Laurel Canyon. I had my car window down and a band called Alvvays playing, loud enough for the teenage girl in the convertible beside me to hear. She smiled and gave me a thumbs-up. Her hair was dark, like Janis's, and her smile reminded me of a photo I'd seen in the bedroom the day Anna told me the news. One in which Janis was smiling. I thought of all the smiles and songs and sunny days the murdered girl would never enjoy now.

The screen on my dash lit up with an incoming call.

"How's the investigation going, Mister Chance?" It was Isabelle Greer calling.

"Inching along. Paige claims he only met Janis one time, and that it's a lie they were dating."

"You spoke to him?"

"And his father."

"I told you she might have made it up."

"Well, someone is lying."

She went silent.

"Did she liked to be called Janis or Jan?" I asked.

"Janis. Nobody called her Jan more than once. She hated it and let you know." Another pause.

"Did you have a specific reason for calling, Isabelle? I only say that because I'm in the canyon and might lose you."

"I've just been contemplating things. Her death. How sad it makes me." There was a somber, mature quality to her voice now, as if she'd aged a few years in the time since I last saw her. "What if Billie really did do it?"

"Do you think she's capable of something so horrific?" I said.

"That fight I saw was pretty intense. When she said she hated her sister's guts, I believed her. And she could go pretty dark, was into all that goth stuff. She liked to watch these really sick movies, like the *Exorcist* and stuff by David Lynch."

"A lot of people like both those things, Isabelle. It doesn't mean they're murderers."

"She listened to some really scary music, too."

"Give me some examples."

"Marilyn Manson. I mean, come on. He's freaky. And a band called The Horrors. Oh, and this old one. The Cure. She loved them."

The Cure. Like in Kathy's dream.

"Not everyone who listens to dark music is a killer, either," I said.

"I'm just trying to paint a picture for you. Billie talked a lot about death. How she didn't understand the world, and the world didn't understand her, and sometimes she wanted to kill herself. She usually sounded a lot older than she was. I think her dad's death a few years ago did a real number on her, and she never recovered. Janis's reaction was to go wild when he got killed. Billie's was to go dark, dark, dark."

"Well, thank you for your insight. I appreciate it."

"No problem. I like talking to you, Mister Chance. You don't treat me like a little girl, the way a lot of adults do. Will you call me and keep me up to date? Tell me how things are going?"

"As much as I feel I can."

"Cool." She waited for me to say more. I didn't. "Okay, well, goodbye."

"Goodbye, Isabelle. And thank you."

She ended the call.

Almost immediately, my phone rang again. *KATHY CALLING* lit up the screen.

"What's up, Katbird?" I said, answering.

"It's Charley," she said. "Something's wrong."

10

"Charley's not answering or opening," Kathy told me, standing outside our bedroom door. "And it's locked."

I jiggled the handle; it had been secured from the inside. "Charley, it's me," I said, and tapped three times on the wood.

No response.

"Get me a flathead screwdriver," I told Kathy. She hurried off to the kitchen. I knocked again, more forcefully. "Charley, I'm going to force open the door, and then I'm coming in." I mentally fought off worst-case scenarios of what I'd find inside.

Kathy returned and handed me the tool. I wedged the tip between the door and the jamb, scraping it against the wood, not caring what damage I did. Once it found the sweet spot between the latch and the strike plate, I torqued the screwdriver to the left, pushing the latch back into its cylinder. Then I eased the door inward and stepped into a dark room. Charley lay on the bed, her back to the door.

"Charley?"

She didn't respond or move.

"Is she okay?" Kathy asked.

"I don't know."

I crossed to the other side of the bed where I could see Charley's face. Her eyes were closed, her mouth open in a small O. I lifted her wrist and checked for a pulse, relieved to feel a steady, rhythmic flow of blood. Her skin was warm and damp with sweat. I looked over at the nightstand. Its top was littered with containers of cream and burn treatment medications: a tub of silver sulfadiazine, a water mister, a prescription bottle of the anti-anxiety drug Ativan—lorazepam, its generic name, is commonly used for burn treatment as an adjunct to opioid analgesics like morphine sulfate, of which there was also a pill bottle. This last one was open and on its side. Several tablets had fallen out.

THE PARAMEDICS ARRIVED IN LESS THAN FIFTEEN MINUTES. They checked Charley's vitals and put an oxygen mask over her mouth and nose. Respiratory difficulty, I learned, was a common side effect of mixing morphine and lorazepam. "Most likely she took too much of one or the other by accident," one paramedic told me.

After a few breaths of fresh, pure oxygen in her lungs, Charley opened her eyes. She seemed disoriented, fearful, and reached for the mask to pull it off. I put a hand on her forearm to stop her.

"It's okay," I said. "You passed out. A bad interaction, they think. You were having trouble breathing, so you need to leave the mask on for a while."

She looked up at me, confused, then glanced over at the

pill bottles on the nightstand. Her eyes teared. "I got mixed up," she said, her voice muted through the plastic cover. "Couldn't remember which one I'd taken. Thought I'd forgotten one. Must have downed an extra." She shook her head. "So stupid."

"It happens more often than you think," the second paramedic said. "Don't be too hard on yourself."

"What do we need to do?" I asked him.

"We'll take her in, have her monitored in the ER for a few hours. If things improve—and there's no reason to think they won't—the on-call doctor will possibly let you bring her back home this evening. But they might want to keep her overnight, just to be safe."

"I don't want to go to the ER," Charley said. Again, she tried to take off the mask.

"It's not your call," I told her. "We don't want to take any chances."

She turned away, slipping her hand out of my grasp.

Kathy and I followed the ambulance to St. Joseph's hospital in Burbank. By the time we'd parked and walked to the emergency room, Charley had been taken to a cubicle in the inner examination center. I filled out forms and answered questions at the admitting desk. Kathy paced anxiously around the waiting room. Once I'd finished and we were ready to go in, a nurse named Ross informed us, kindly but firmly, that Charley made clear she wanted no visitors. When I started to argue, Kathy put a hand on my arm.

"Dad, it's okay," she said. "You know Charley's having all kinds of crazy thoughts right now. She's embarrassed and scared. Probably ashamed, too. She needs a chance to pull herself together. And some space to feel like shit and not have to cover in front of us."

My daughter's insight and wisdom has always impressed me. I nodded and kissed her forehead.

"I'm going to hang around anyway," I said. "In case she changes her mind."

"Well, if you're staying," Kathy said, "then I am, too."

We sat in the waiting room. Kathy texted on her phone and I looked around at a collection of people in pain: a mother barely out of her teens sat with a young girl of perhaps seven who looked feverish, her head resting on her mother's lap while the young parent ran fingers through the child's hair; an elderly couple in matching red sweaters, holding hands and looking fearful; a young woman with a large welt around her left eye who kept her gaze focused on her lap while the man beside her looked annoyed and indifferent. I could imagine any number of scenarios for the waiting patients, but it would all be speculation. We never know the secrets of others until they tell us. Often not even then. As a cop, I've tried to develop useful intuition, but intuition is not truth. And truth will sometimes hide in furtive places.

Had Charley's injuries—and the ordeal that led to them —damaged her even more profoundly than I realized? In trying to act strong and normal, in attempting to face things on her own and get through it all, had she lost clarity? Had her mind betrayed her, while her heart closed itself off? If so, the blame again came back to me.

My cell rang. I stepped outside to answer the call from Anna.

"Billie's regained consciousness," she said. "She's talking, barely though."

"That's good news," I told her.

"She says she doesn't remember anything about the

night Janis was killed. She doesn't even seem aware her sister is dead."

"Do you believe her?"

"It's common with traumatic events that induce shocked states like hers to have no memory of it."

"That's not an answer to my question," I said. "Do you believe she's being honest?"

"Yes."

"Contact Detective Caruso, immediately, and tell him."

"The police will be all over the poor girl once they know. I want some time alone with her."

"Holding back, even for a few hours, is risky, Anna. They may suspect you used the time to coax her."

"Then I'll lie about when she actually regained consciousness."

"That could easily come back to haunt you. And Billie will be the one to suffer for it. Please, do as I advise. They've still got an officer posted outside the house, right?"

"Yes."

"Go tell him now. He'll relay the information to Caruso."

"What about you? Can you come over? Can you talk to her with me? If you can corroborate what she says, that'll make things easier, won't it?"

"Not really," I said. "They might argue I helped you with what she should say. I'll come only after Caruso's seen her. Contact me once he arrives. I'm in the middle of something personal that requires all my attention right now. I'll be there as soon as I can get away. It may not be tonight."

Back in the waiting area, Kathy told me she'd learned they were going to keep Charley for the night. Ironically, the decision was not based on the negative interaction of the morphine and the Ativan that adversely affected her respiratory system and caused her to pass out. During the exam, the doctor noticed an infection developing at one of the burn sites and contacted her dermatologist. They agreed to keep her overnight, administer to the infection, and monitor her recovery.

"We can't stay here all night," Kathy said. "And I doubt Charley's going to change her mind about letting us in to see her between now and morning. Hopefully she'll sleep straight through. And we're ten minutes away if anything changes."

I agreed. She gave me a hug. It felt good.

As we headed back home, I told Kathy that Billie had regained consciousness.

"Is that good news?" Kathy said.

"What would be bad about it?"

"If it turned out she was guilty and knew it."

"I hope that's not the case," I said.

"Me too."

"Did Janis ever mention a guy named Paige Leary?"

Kathy didn't have to think long about this. "A couple of times, yeah. I remember because the name always made me think she was talking about a girl. I wonder if he resents his parents for it."

"What did she tell you about him?"

"That they were dating, and that she thought she was falling in love. Oh, and that it was a secret."

A secret Janis shared with her friends but not her mom.

"Did you ever meet him?" I asked. "Ever see them together?"

"No." She paused. "I met his younger brother once. Wyatt."

"Where did he you meet him?" I asked. "How?"

"He was with Billie at the Commons in Calabasas. They seemed pretty close."

Interesting. Two Learys connected to the Rykers. I wondered if Anna knew about Wyatt's friendship with Billie.

"I've met Paige," I said, "but not Wyatt. No one seems to know where he is."

Kathy typed something onto her phone screen. "That's him," she said. The soft face of a, and showed me the screen. I stared at the face of a teenager, skinny and marred by acne, his blonde hair a mess. There was a haunted look in his eyes. It reminded me of the expression I saw repeatedly in the photos of Billie. I understood from that single look the connection between the two and why, despite the age difference, they'd become friends.

BACK AT THE HOUSE, I CLOSED MY STUDY DOOR, TURNED OFF the light and shut the blinds, then took off my shoes and sat in my favorite chair to meditate. I'd been doing Transcendental Meditation for some time—thanks to Anna Ryker. She'd turned me on to it at the end of the Nora Lord murder investigation. I was hesitant when she first suggested I start, skeptical even, and it took a while for me to ease into the practice. Now the twice-a-day, 20-minute dive into tranquility has become indispensable to me. It clears my head, energizes my body, and brings balance to my life. Or at least as much balance as possible to someone whose main purpose is to investigate death.

When I'd finished, I called the hospital to check on Charley. Ross, the same nurse I'd spoken with earlier, assured me she was breathing comfortably without the oxygen mask and had been given antibiotics for the infection. She would most likely sleep through the night, he said. I thanked him and signed off. I debated calling Caruso to find out if Anna had taken my advice and let him know that Billie had regained consciousness. Then Kathy knocked on the study door with news that changed everything.

11

I followed Kathy into the entrance foyer. Anna stood just inside the front door. Billie was at her side, hands clasped in front of her, eyes cast down, mouth in a pout. The young girl's black hair was wet and slicked back on her scalp. If she'd seemed pale when I last saw her, she looked pallid and anemic now. I held back from reprimanding Anna in front of her daughter. Instead, I crouched down so Billie and I were at the same level.

"Hi Billie," I said. "We've never met. I'm Jason. I've known your mother for several years."

"Mr. Chance is helping us, baby," Anna said, a hand on her daughter's shoulder. "Like I told you in the car. You don't have to be afraid of him."

Billie looked at me, then over at Kathy, wordlessly.

"Would you like something to drink?" I asked. "Water? Some juice? A soda, maybe? Kathy can get you something." Billie shrugged, dropping her gaze back to her hands. I told Kathy to take Billie to the kitchen and get her a ginger ale. "Would you like some tea?" I asked Anna.

"Yes. Thank you. Any kind you have."

Kathy nodded and led Billie off. The young girl gave no resistance.

"I'm sorry," Anna said. "I know this is wildly inappropriate. Nothing I'm doing is at all in character, it seems." She attempted a laugh. It came out as more of a cackle, something that made her seem close to hysteria. "I'm having trouble even remembering what *character* means lately."

"How did you get away from the house and the policemen?" I asked.

"We went out through the kitchen and up to Marty and Lenny's house," Anna said. "From there, I called an Uber. And I know what you're going to say. But I got scared, Jason. Scared Caruso would take her in if he learned she'd regained consciousness."

"He couldn't do that. It would be violating a judge's order. Now, though, by running, you've given him the power. You're the one in violation. You've made things much worse."

"I didn't think. I just acted." She wrapped her arms around her waist, as if in pain, and leaned back against the hallway wall.

"Billie remembers nothing?" I said.

"Nothing past feeling sick at Caitlyn's house and lying down."

"How much have you told her?"

"Only that Janis is dead. I couldn't keep the news from her. And I needed to be certain she heard it from me."

"How does she think it happened?"

"An intruder came into the house."

"Her reaction?"

"She didn't have one, which is disturbing. She seemed numb to the news. I don't think it's sunk in yet. It's clear she doesn't remember finding the body."

"You've got to take her back to the house, Anna. You might still be able to salvage this. You don't want to make Caruso your enemy."

"He already is."

Before I could respond, Billie called, "Mom," from the other room.

Anna hurried down the corridor. I followed. Billie stood in the living room, by the patio door, looking around like a frightened animal in foreign terrain.

"What's wrong, sweetie?" Anna said.

"I thought I saw something outside. Like a shadow or a figure against the back wall."

I stepped to the patio door and flicked a switch on the wall. The lamps in the backyard lit up, shining light across the grass, from the deck to the retaining wall.

"There's nobody there," Anna said. "See?"

"You probably saw the shadow of a tree," I said. "In darkness, it can look ominous. And sometimes we get raccoons and possums back there."

"I'm scared," Billie said, though her voice sounded calm. "He's gonna come for me next, isn't he?"

"Who?" I said.

"The man who killed Janis. Does he want to kill me, too?"

Anna crossed to her daughter and knelt in front of her. "No, sweetheart. No one wants to kill you. What happened to Janis was a terrible thing. But I'm not going to let anyone hurt you. Ever. Do you understand?" She led her daughter to the sofa. They sat.

"Someone killed my sister," Billie said, matter-of-factly, looking at me.

"I know. I'm sorry."

"Mom says I was asleep for three days after it happened.

But it feels to me like I fell asleep last night at the party and woke up today in my bed. Like it's only been one night."

"What is the last thing you remember?" I asked.

"Telling my friend Caitlyn that I didn't feel well. She said I could go lie down in her room if I wanted."

"Did you?"

"Yeah."

"What was wrong?"

"My head hurt. I felt nauseous."

"Had you had anything to drink at the party?"

Billie fidgeted, glancing over at Anna. "Yeah, with Caitlyn. A shot of tequila. Maybe two. And a beer."

My cell buzzed in my pocket, loud enough to cause Billie to flinch. "Sorry," I said. Thinking it might be news about Charley, I took the phone out and looked at the screen. It read: *Dante Caruso Calling.*

"Do you need to take that?" Anna asked.

"Probably better if I don't, right now." I hit ignore and set the phone aside.

Kathy entered from the kitchen, carrying a small tray that held two mugs of steaming tea and two cans of ginger ale. Once she'd handed out the drinks, I said to her, "Do me a favor, call and check on things with Charley. I want to make sure she's comfortable."

Kathy gave me a thumbs-up, then excused herself and left the room.

"Is everything okay?" Anna asked.

"Nothing you need to concern yourself with," I said, and turned to look at Billie. "I'd like to ask you a few questions about Janis, if I may." There would be hell to pay if Caruso found out I'd questioned her before he'd had the chance, but she was here now, and I might not get another opportunity.

Billie shrugged, glancing at her mother.

"It's okay, honey. Tell Jason anything he wants to know. He's trying to help us."

"Okay," she said, twisting her fingers around each other.

"You and your sister had an argument a while ago, in the school parking lot. Do you remember that?"

Billie hesitated. Her hands had gone still. I felt I'd caught her off guard. "Kind of," she said.

"What exactly was the fight about?"

"Just sister stuff. You know. I didn't like the way she'd been acting lately."

"And how had she been acting?"

"She was being mean. To me. To Mom."

"Someone told me you called her a slut."

Billie furrowed her brow and shook her head. "No, it wasn't like that."

"That you said, 'You're embarrassing Mom, and you're embarrassing yourself.' You don't remember that?"

"Why are you asking me? What does it have to do with Janis getting killed?"

"I'm trying to help find whoever was responsible. Maybe it was someone she knew. Someone she might have been dating, perhaps."

"Janis didn't have a boyfriend," Billie said.

"What about Paige Leary?"

"What's he got to do with this?"

"You never heard Janis talk about him? Say she was dating him?"

"I don't believe that ever happened," Anna said, before Billie could respond.

Billie popped the top on the can of ginger ale and drank.

"You and Paige's brother, Wyatt, are pretty close, aren't you?" I said.

"I don't know what this has to do with anything," Billie said. "Can we go now, Mom? Your friend is waiting."

"What friend?" I asked, turning to Anna.

"Billie is confused," Anna said. "I told her we were going to see a friend and I meant you. Here."

"Oh," Billie said with a scowl. "My mistake." She then reached for something in her back pocket. "Shit."

"Billie, language," Anna said.

"What's wrong?" I asked.

"My phone," Billie said. "I think I left it at home. Or maybe it fell out in the Uber. What am I going to do?"

"They'll put it in their lost and found and we'll get it tomorrow," Anna said.

Billie grew quiet and looked disturbed.

"I'd like to step outside for a few minutes and finish talking with your mom," I said, "if that's okay."

Billie ignored me and went back to searching her pockets, as if the device might miraculously reappear. I slid open the patio door and let Anna exit before me. The evening was warm and a little humid, a change from the predawn chill Charley and I'd enjoyed that morning. Crickets chirped. The sprinklers in the back lawn were spritzing with a low hiss.

"The hissing of summer lawns," Anna said of the sound, using the title of an old Joni Mitchell album. "Joni was playing on the sound system in my office when we first met, remember?"

"Who is the friend waiting for you, Anna?"

"I told you, Billie was confused." She stared out across the yard.

I let the lie go. "Did you have a chance to look at your files regarding those dates in August?" I asked.

"No. I was going to do it this evening, but then Billie woke up and everything changed."

"Did you know about Billie's friendship with Wyatt Leary?"

Anna shook her head. "How did you learn about it?"

"Kathy saw them together once. She said they seemed very close."

"You tell yourself you know all the important things about your children, but you never do. It's all a mystery."

"Is it possible she said his name the other night in her sleep?" I said. "Not *why not* but *Wyatt*."

"I suppose. What does it matter?"

"Maybe it doesn't. But Kathy said Janis told her she'd been dating Paige, and that it was a secret. He called her Jan when we spoke, which to me implies a certain intimacy. There's a connection between Paige's younger brother and Billie. I'm on to something here, Anna. You must go back home so I can stay on it. Maybe you can sneak back in and the guards outside will never even know you left."

"Don't you get it, Jason? Caruso's not going to believe Billie doesn't remember. He doesn't care what you may be on to. He's been giving you lip service. He could've found out everything you've learned in two days. He just doesn't want to. He's already made up his mind about her."

"Then go home for Billie's sake. A judge believed you would follow the law in taking care of her. You've violated the bail agreement by sneaking out of your house. They could put her back in jail because of this."

"The minute I tell Caruso she's awake, he'll be all over her with questions, and then his court-appointed psychiatrists will go after her. She'll be scared. She'll get confused. They'll make her say things that sound incriminating. Because it's what they want. I won't let that happen. I'm a mother before I'm a doctor. I'm not going to let the system destroy her." The intensity in her voice—the vehemence—came, I knew, from desperation, and it troubled me. Desperate people do desperate things. And they make foolish mistakes.

"You didn't come here tonight for help, did you?" I said. "You came to say goodbye. You're running away."

Anna stared at me for a long time, terror in her eyes she couldn't mask.

"Don't do it," I said. "Please."

"I never should've brought you in. I should've handled it on my own from the beginning." She slid the patio door open and re-entered the house. "Come on, Billie," she said. "We have to go."

The young girl looked up nervously.

"Don't do something you'll later regret," I said.

"I already have," Anna said, then took Billie by the hand and led her out of the living room, down the hallway, and out of the house.

I HAD TROUBLE SLEEPING THAT NIGHT. I LAY ON MY SIDE, staring out the window. A shadow on the side property wall looked in the darkness like some creature rising from the ground. I wondered if it was the same shadow that had frightened Billie.

The image made me think of a song by the Police, "Synchronicity II," the lyrics comparing the shadow of a monster on the door of a Loch Ness cottage with the rage that builds up in every human being at one point or another. Rage propelled Janis's killer, as it had with so many crimes I'd investigated. Anna felt rage at a world of which she felt she'd lost control. And God knows what anger, beyond the normal explosion of teenage hormones, might be festering inside Billie. For all her internal angst and soft manner, she felt to me like a bomb ready to detonate. Maybe she already had. Maybe Janis paid the price for that.

The horrors of being human cripple us, not fears of the end of the world.

Around 3 a.m., my phone alerted me to an incoming text. Hoping it might be from Charley, I sat up, turned on the light, and picked up the device. The message across the screen consisted of one sentence.

now look what you did.

I opened my messages app to see the incoming number. It had an 818-area code—local—but was not a number I recognized. I typed *who is this?* and sent the reply.

A moment later, another text came through:

i'm the one u should b looking 4.

I typed *what do you want?*

The texter responded *you'll find out soon enough* followed by a laughing emoji and the words *sleep tite.*

12

I called the number. No one answered, and no voicemail greeting kicked in. I ended the call and set my phone aside. The text comments were vague but disturbing. A prank? Possibly.

Let it go, Jason. It doesn't mean anything. A kid playing a game. Probably sent to the wrong number.

I turned off the light, lay back down, and closed my eyes. Eventually sleep came, though not without a struggle, and it kept its hold on me until almost eight in the morning. Kathy had gone for a run, leaving a note by the coffeemaker. I called to check on Charley and was put on hold before I'd even had a chance to state the purpose of my call. After waiting five minutes, I hung up, deciding I'd go over and check on her in person, once visiting hours began.

I poured myself half a cup of coffee and drank it black while checking my phone to see if the mysterious texter had sent another message while I slept. Nothing had come in—more proof the texts were probably not important. I went into the study, closed the door, and did my morning meditation.

Later, out on the deck with a second cup of coffee and a breakfast bar, I watched as a pair of robins danced across the back lawn, looking for worms in the grass and dirt. One of the birds eventually grew bored and flew off. The other jumped up on the deck railing and watched me as I sipped coffee and ate my breakfast. Feeling generous, I broke off a small piece of granola and tossed it down onto the grass. The bird swooped after it, picked up the morsel in its beak, gulped it down, and looked back at me appreciatively. I was about to toss another morsel when a new text flashed on the screen of my phone:

you took me seriously, right?

A few seconds passed, then another one came:

i'm no hoax.

I typed *tell me who you are and what you want.*

The texter went silent. I opened the message app and scrolled through the bizarre exchange. What last night seemed like a prank now felt ominous and worthy of attention. I called a friend in the sheriff's department Internet and telecommunications division. We chatted about my leave of absence, about the woman's decision to relocate to San Diego at the end of the year to be closer to her mother, and a little about the upcoming lineup at the *Lollapalooza* music festival in Chicago. All warm-up schmooze building to the real purpose of my call: a favor.

"This gonna get me in trouble?" she asked.

"Not if nobody knows. It's a simple cell phone tracking request. I need to know who a number that's been harassing me belongs to."

The woman chuckled. "Some woman you dumped? How's Charley, by the way?"

"Better than ever," I lied. "And the texts aren't from someone I know. At least I don't think they are."

"You should report this."

"Can you get me the ID first?"

"Only because it's you, Jason. Give me a bit and I'll call you back."

Ten minutes later, I had the information I wanted.

The texts had come from a phone number on the Verizon network registered to Anna Ryker.

There were three phones registered to Doctor Ryker's plan. I recognized one as her personal number. The other two I assumed belonged to her daughters. The texts had come from the second oldest one on the account, meaning the phone probably belonged to Janis. Anna hadn't mentioned that Janis's cell had gone missing after the murder. It could be she didn't know, had never bothered to check. But Caruso should have, and he'd not said anything about it. Maybe the theft had occurred during the break-in at Anna's office. Or maybe Janis lost it long before the killing.

i'm the one u should b looking 4.

Should I call Caruso? Anna's illegal flight with Billie had, for all intents and purposes, canceled out my investigation. And there was always the possibility these texts had come from Billie herself, as an attempt at deflection. I needed more information.

First, though, I needed to check on Charley.

I parked in the St. Joseph's lot and entered the emergency room through the visitor's door. A new nurse sat behind the reception window. I identified myself and said

I'd come to check on a patient admitted the night before. "Charlotte Frasier."

The woman typed Charlotte's name into her computer, waited as info popped up, then said, "She checked herself out this morning."

The news threw me. "Are you sure? Maybe the doctor relocated her to the main hospital."

"No sir. The main hospital is where she spent the night. She's definitely gone now."

I stepped outside and called Charley's cell. It went straight to voicemail. "Charley, it's me. I'm here at the hospital. What's going on? Where are you? Call me back."

Looking around, I spotted Ross, the nurse from the night before, heading across the lot. I jogged over, catching him before he got into his car.

"Good morning," I said. "Remember me?"

"Mister Chance, of course. What's up?"

"Were you around when Charlotte Frasier was released this morning?"

"Yeah, the doctor gave her the okay to leave about an hour ago," he said. "I was just finishing my shift."

"Did you happen to talk to her before she left?"

"Only to say goodbye."

"How did she seem?"

Ross paused, studying me, and then said, "Look, Mister Chance, I don't know what the deal is between the two of you. And I don't know how she got those burns. It's none of my business. Any of it. But it seems she's sending a message that you might want to pay attention to." He got into his car, pulling the door shut. His engine revved, and he drove off.

I called Kathy. "Have you heard from Charley?"

"No. What's wrong?"

"She checked herself out."

"Seriously? She's not here, and she hasn't called."

"I'm going to her apartment."

"Dad, don't. I mean it. I know this is hard for you. It's hard for me, too. But she obviously wants to be alone right now. You've got to give her some time. Please."

This time I ignored her advice and drove to the West Hollywood apartment Charley had held onto even though she'd moved back in with Kathy and me. She didn't respond at first to my buzzing the intercom from the front door, but I kept at it, pushing the button on the box by the entrance until I finally heard a weak voice from the speaker.

"Jagger?" she said.

"Who else? Buzz me in. I won't stay long. I just need to see that you're okay."

"Anything but."

"Let me up," I said.

The door buzzed open. I took the stairs two at a time to the second floor. Her apartment was just off the stairwell, its door ajar to allow me entry on my own. Inside, the lights of the apartment were off and the window curtains closed. I saw the faint silhouette of Charley sitting on the sofa, her back to me.

"I'm sorry if I frightened you," she said. "I thought about calling, but I talked myself out of it. I'm not even sure why." Her voice was soft, apathetic. "I guess I didn't want you to follow me here. I should've known you would, anyway."

Approaching, I saw a thin plastic burn mask covering her face. Her left shoulder and neck were bandaged with moist gauze. She had a mug of tea in her hand.

"The pill thing was careless," she said. "Stupid. I got confused."

"There's no judgment here. No blame."

"There's plenty of blame, Jagger."

"Then I hope it's all directed at me."

"No." She turned to face me, her eyes barely visible through the holes of the mask. "Believe it or not, you're off the hook."

"I shouldn't be."

"Does it matter? It is what it is. I need to learn to live with the aftermath. It's just proving harder to do than I thought it would be. Last night it hit home that I'm still closer to the beginning than the end of this ordeal, and that depresses the shit out of me."

"So you shouldn't push away the two people who love you more than anything else in this world."

"Don't make this about you," she said.

"I'm not trying to. But I'm in the dark here and I'm scared."

Charley let loose a furious cry and threw the mug against the wall. It shattered. The pieces fell to the floor. Wet tea dripped down the wall. "I can't do this," she whispered. She slumped back into her chair. "Everything's changed."

I stood still, trying to think how best to proceed. I probably should have heeded Kathy's advice and given Charley more room. *Jagger the Jerk* strikes again.

"I'm sorry," Charley said. "I guess irrational and uncontrollable anger is another side effect."

"I don't blame you for being angry. You got dealt a shitty hand and now we need to pull you through it, together. We need to figure things out, together. We're supposed to be getting married. Nothing's changed about that, has it?"

"I need time. I don't know how much."

"Charley ..."

"Go, Jagger," she said. "Please, just ... go."

She stood, walked into her bedroom without looking at me, and shut the door. I wanted to follow her. To grab her and rip the plastic mask off her face, to kiss her blistered lips. To make clear to her she couldn't get rid of me. But I knew it would be a mistake, the worst kind under the circumstances. Kathy was right. Charley needed to go through all the stages of recovery, the emotional as well as the physical, and she had to do it in her own way and at her own pace. It was selfish to think I knew better.

"I love you," I called out, and then left the apartment, closing the door behind me.

Driving back to the valley, I played Augustana's *All the Stars and Boulevards* as loudly as the car speakers could handle. My hands gripped the steering wheel so tightly my knuckles hurt. A ringing in my ears blocked out much of the blaring music. Finally, I pulled over to the curb and shut the motor off. I muted the speakers and rolled down the windows so I could hear noise and life and the city, hoping it would help bring the world back into focus. Instead, a simple message from the mysterious texter lit up the screen of my phone:

i've done it again.

13

An LAPD patrol car with two uniformed officers inside was parked in front of my house when I returned, right behind Caruso's beige Crown Victoria. I pulled into my driveway, shut off the engine, and watched in the rearview mirror as Dante got out of his car. Simply doing it seemed a struggle for him.

"Where are they, Chance?" he said, approaching across the lawn. "What's going on?"

I got out and faced him. "They're not here."

"Then where'd they go?" His chin and cheeks were dark with stubble, his eyes bloodshot. I smelled sweat beneath his cologne. He looked like he'd had a rough night.

"Come inside," I said. "Your cops can sit tight. I'm not hiding the Rykers, and this won't take long."

Caruso motioned for the patrolmen to stay put. He followed me into the house.

"I don't know where they are," I said, leading him back to the living room. "But Anna came to see me last night. Billie was with her. The girl's regained consciousness. She claims she doesn't remember anything after the party she attended."

"Of course not." If there was a better word than "skeptical" for his expression, I couldn't come up with it. "You didn't think to do the right thing and call me?"

"I did think about it. But I got pulled into a private situation that took precedence. This is not my case, remember?"

"But Anna Ryker came straight to you. Three times, now. First, after the arrest. Then, after the so-called break-in at her place. And last night, before she decided to disappear. You seem to be here go-to guy."

"Last night, I urged her to call you. It's not my fault she slipped past your men."

He rubbed a hand across his mouth as if trying to wipe away some stain, then let it slide down to scratch his throat. "I can't for the life of me figure you out, Chance. I believe you're a smart cop, but I don't know where the hell you really are in all this."

I took out my phone and called up the texts I'd received. "These were sent to me last night. The phone number is registered to Anna Ryker, one of three accounts in her name. Based on the date of activation, I'm assuming the messages are coming from Janis's phone."

Caruso read through the texts. "Well, they're sure not coming from Janis. Must be the little sister. Or maybe the mom. A lame attempt to throw off suspicion."

"I find it highly unlikely Anna would stoop that low."

"Then it's Billie."

"The phone could have been stolen by whomever broke into Anna's house and office," I said.

"Yeah, about that. My team went through her place. Again. Top to bottom. No locks forced, no windows broken. Nothing different or new from the search we gave it the night Janis Ryker was killed. The robbery story is about as believable as these texts."

"Anna's smarter than that."

"You know what your problem is, Chance? You've got too much faith in people."

"And you've lost all faith in everyone because you're dying. Which one is worse?"

He shook his head, barely grinning. "I was even starting to like you." He turned to go, then stopped and glanced back. "If you know where they are, or if Mrs. Ryker gave you even the slightest indication as to where they're headed, and you don't tell me, you're aiding and abetting. I won't think twice about arresting you."

"I'll keep that in mind," I said.

He frowned. "Ever consider the possibility that she's using you?"

"Not for a second."

"It's her only surviving child," Caruso said. "She'll do whatever she thinks she has to. And I don't blame her. But I've gotta do what I've gotta do, as well. Which is bring them in. They're both fugitives now. If they get in touch with you, please let me know."

I tried to think of a strong and clever thing to say, some great parting words, but I came up empty. Everything he'd said was true. They were fugitives. If I helped them, I was guilty, too. And maybe I was a fool to still have any faith.

Caruso walked out the door.

"Who was that?" Kathy asked from the foyer.

"The detective investigating Janis's murder. He came looking for them."

"Do you know where they are?"

"No clue. And that's the God's honest truth."

We went into my study. Kathy plopped down on the

small sofa and asked if I'd heard from Charley. I told her I'd gone to see her.

"Dad, I thought we agreed—"

"You suggested. I didn't listen." I sank into my desk chair. "But I should have. It was a mistake. We're going to have to give her some time."

"That's what I've been telling you."

"I know," I said. "You were right. Feel vindicated?"

"No, just sad," she said. "This whole thing sucks."

"It sure does." It dawned on me she shouldn't be home. "Why aren't you at school?"

"I took a sick day. In case Charley needed me."

"That's your way of giving her time and space?"

"Dad, don't even ... I'm here *if* she needs me. I'm not the one breaking down her door."

"A bit of an exaggeration, but point taken."

"How did you two leave things?"

"Not well."

"Dad!" She glared at me.

"It's going to be fine, Katbird. In a day or two. Maybe a little longer."

"If you messed this up—"

"I don't think I did. But if so, I'll fix it."

Kathy didn't seem appeased. She stalked off to her room. I closed the door and took out my cell, calling up the most recent message from my online stalker.

i've done it again.

Opening the laptop on my desk, I did a search of recent Los Angeles murders, using the keywords *stabbing, teenage, kitchen knife, bloody scene, carnage*. I added a date range of the past three days.

A string of links filled the screen:

Man Shot Near Northridge 7-Eleven, Another

Stabbed.

Homeless Man Fatally Knifed by Irate Driver at West Covina Gas Station.

Parents Claim Sweet Sixteen Party Stabbing Was Racially Motivated Hate Crime.

I scrolled down until I found one that seemed to fit the mold.

Seventeen-Year-Old Babysitter Stabbed in Woodland Hills Guest House.

I clicked on this link. An LA Times article from that morning popped open, filling the computer screen.

Jo Kensington July 18, 2018 | 8:05 A.M.

Parents of eight-year-old Bethany Stewart walked into a bloody scene early Wednesday morning when they found seventeen-year-old babysitter Natalie Cara of Canoga Park dead in the guest house of their Woodland Hills home on Valerie Avenue. They'd returned from dinner and a show at the Pantages Theater in Hollywood. After searching the main house, they discovered the young girl's naked body on the bed of the converted garage, tied to the bed posts with leather belts taken from Mr. Stewart's bedroom. She'd been stabbed repeatedly in the torso and abdomen. Their daughter, Bethany was unharmed, asleep in her own room. The victim is the only child of Ignacio and Gloria Cara of Canoga Park. Neither the Caras nor the Stewarts were available for comment.

I sat back and stared at a high school yearbook photograph of the young victim. She had dark, curly hair and light brown eyes. Her smile in the picture was filled with exhilaration and optimism. A hopeful future had been cut short by an assassin's hand. Was this related? Was it what my texter meant by *I've done it again*? It was the only local crime reported that bore any similarities to Janis's murder.

The details of the killing were reminiscent. But not an exact match.

I copied the URL for the article and emailed it to Caruso, with a note telling him about the latest text. It would interest Caruso or it wouldn't. I remained resolved to let him deal with the investigation from here on out.

Another text came in just after midnight:
i'm not her u forced me to do this.

I tapped the info icon in the top right corner, then the phone icon on the subsequent screen. The call rang but no one answered, and no voicemail, just as before. I got up and went into the bathroom, splashed my face with cold water. In the kitchen, I made a cup of tea. Sitting at the kitchen table, sipping the hot beverage, I rereading the last message. *I'm not her* referred, I assumed, to Billie. Did the next statement—*you forced me to do this*—refer to the texts, or to killing Natalie Cara? It's very difficult to pick up the sentiment behind the phrasing of a text, but these words felt threatening.

I set the phone down and rubbed my dry, burning eyes. Exhaustion was creeping back in. I finished the tea, leaned back in the chair, and closed my eyes to rest them. The next thing I knew, a gentle shaking woke me and it was early morning, the first rays of light creating a gray glow in the windows. Kathy stood at my side, her open laptop computer in her hand.

"You need to see this," she said, and put the computer on the table.

It took a moment for the haze of sleep to clear. I leaned toward the computer to see what was on the screen: an email addressed to Kathy, from billieryker@gmail.com. The subject line was empty, and there were six sentences in the message box:

I'm scared. I don't know what to do. Mom is acting crazy. Why did she come to see your dad? She won't tell me anything or even let me watch TV. Is it about Janis? What's going on?

"You just got this?" I asked.

Kathy nodded. "Ten minutes ago."

I looked at the clock on the kitchen wall. It was just past 6 a.m.

"What should I do?" Kathy asked.

"Nothing. It's not your place to tell her she's a murder suspect. And what else could you say? Besides, if she has a computer or a phone to send that email, and she's so curious, chances are she already knows."

"Then why pretend she doesn't?"

"That's the million-dollar question," I said. "But it's not our problem. I know that sounds cold, but Anna has made it impossible for me to continue helping her. She fled. They're on their own."

Kathy nodded, then glanced down at my phone. The screen had just come to life. "You've got a new text," she said.

I picked up the device and looked at the message, center-screen.

i know where they r.

Kathy looked down over my shoulder at the screen. "What's that about?"

"Someone's been sending me texts. Strange and disturbing ones." I opened the message app and handed the phone to Kathy. She sat across from me and scrolled up to the top of the sequence, then read aloud the texter's messages.

"*Now look what you did.*" She paused, looking up. "This next one is from you? Asking, *who is this?*"

I nodded.

Kathy kept reading. "*Maybe I'm the one you're looking for.* Then you, *what do you want?* Answer, *you'll find out soon enough.*" She swiped her finger across the screen and continued to read. "*I've done it again. I'm not her. You forced me to do this.* Then, *I know where they are.*" She set the phone down. "These are insane. Any idea who they're from?"

"They were sent from Janis's phone," I said.

"The killer stole her phone and is texting you? Bragging?"

"It seems like it. At least it's what the texter wants me to think."

"Why draw attention? The police are focused on Billie. If I'm the real killer, why would I want to take suspicion off her?"

"Maybe Billie's sending them to throw me off. That's what Caruso believes."

"Do you?"

"No."

Kathy tapped the home button to wake the phone back up and read the last message. "*I know where they are* sounds like a threat."

"It sure does."

14

A squad car sat in front of Anna's house, two uniformed policemen side-by-side in the front seat. They weren't there to guard but to arrest—on the off-chance Anna decided to return with Billie. I cruised past them, my head lowered and turned away, the visor of my cap pulled down to my brow. The house Marty Astor shared with his husband Lenny was at the bend in the road just before the cul-de-sac. I parked in front of it, out of the view of the officers below, and hurried across the lawn to their front door.

Lenny opened after a couple of knocks. He looked surprised, his body tensing. "Detective Chance? Has something happened to Anna and Billie?"

"I hope not," I said. "May I come in?" He stepped aside, glancing at the street as I passed him. "It's okay. I don't think the cops saw me."

The house smelled of food: roasting chicken and caramelized Brussel sprouts. Jazz played from small speakers on the mantel above the fireplace.

"Martin," Lenny called out. "Your detective friend is here."

Marty entered from the kitchen, wiping his hands on an orange apron tied around his waist. "Detective Chance. Oh God, please don't tell me you're bringing us more bad news."

"I need to find Anna," I said. "If she told you where she was headed or gave you any indication where she might go, you need to tell me now."

He groaned and leaned back against the door jamb. "She warned me you'd come asking."

"And here I am. Tell me what you can."

"Nothing," Marty said. His face turned a dark shade of red.

"You're lying."

"For God's sake, Marty," Lenny said. He seemed upset about the whole situation. When I'd first met him, he struck me as a man who angered easily and often.

"There is a possibility they may be in danger," I said. "The case has gone in a direction none of us anticipated."

"What does that mean?" Marty said.

"It means you need to tell me where they are."

"With all due respect, Jason, why should I trust you? Anna said you were okay with the police having arrested her."

"That's incorrect. I urged her to let the police do their job. I said she should trust the process."

"How do I know you're not just saying that now so they can find her?"

"Just tell him what he needs to know so we can get back to our lives," Lenny said. "Anna had no right dragging us into this. I love her, I feel for Billie, and what happened to Janis is beyond horrific, but enough is enough."

"I'm sorry the poor girl's death has inconvenienced you so," Marty said to Lenny. He sounded more hurt than angry.

"Save it for later, guys," I said. "I need to find Anna and Billie now."

The two ignored me, their argument escalating. "Don't get melodramatic," Lenny said. "You know I'm right, you just won't admit it."

Marty shook his fists at the ceiling. "Ah! You make me so angry! You didn't want to help Anna in the first place. You acted like you didn't even want them in the house."

"Because I happen to agree with Detective Chance. Turning a thirteen-year-old girl into a fugitive is the worst thing Annie could have done. Let the police do what our taxes pay them to do."

"Guys, stop," I said, more forcefully.

"Sometimes I think *you* believe she's guilty," Marty said. "You're as bad as him!" He pointed at me.

"We don't know the truth, either way," Lenny said.

"She's a little girl," Marty shouted.

"Oh, grow up," Lenny said. "There's no such thing as youthful innocence anymore. It's a whole new world. The Internet changed everything."

"I love you, Lenny," Marty said, "but sometimes you make me so damned mad."

"Enough!" I said. "Both of you, shut up!" The pair went silent. I looked at Marty. "I know you think you're doing the right thing, and that you're protecting them. But their running makes Billie look guilty, and your keeping their whereabouts a secret could be putting them in more danger."

Marty looked bewildered, biting his lip while shaking his head. "Could you please turn that off," he said to Lenny, referring to the music. Lenny stepped over to a stereo system on a nearby bookshelf and flipped a knob. The music stopped. "She said they were heading to the desert," Marty told me, pain etching into his face, a man who felt he'd just committed an atrocious act. "She knows an old friend, a professor from college, who lives there."

"Do you have an address?" I asked.

"No, I swear. That's all she told me."

"A name, at least?"

Marty looked at Lenny. Lenny said, "Tell him."

"Fine! All right! Her name is Catherine. Catherine Zeigler. She lives in Indio, outside Palm Springs."

I WALKED DOWN THE SLOPE FROM MARTY AND LENNY'S HOUSE to Anna's backyard, almost losing my balance on the steep, grassy incline. The lawn behind the Ryker house was overgrown. I jumped over a fallen tire swing and two children's bicycles on the way to the kitchen door. Standing on the small porch, I took off my cap and used it to shield my fist as I shattered a glass pane. I reached in, turned the lock knob, and entered.

The room smelled of grease and day-old cooked food. Dishes were piled up in the sink; dirty pans covered the stove. A bowl of soup, half-eaten, sat on the kitchen table next to an open can of ginger ale. The trashcan by the backdoor was half-filled and stank of garbage. It was as if I'd stepped into a different kitchen than the one I'd last visited. The mess had built up over the course of only a few days. I thought of the Poe story, *The Fall of the House of Usher*, in which a house literally fell into ruin as its main inhabitant deteriorated physically and psychologically. I was seeing the decline of someone I cared for deeply, and it broke my heart.

I went to Anna's office. The three misplaced August session tapes were now back in their correct spots in the cabinet drawer. I took them out and over to Anna's older model mini-DV video camera. The battery of the machine was at three quarters. I opened one of the DV tape boxes, slipped the mini-DV into the camcorder, flipped out a small LCD viewing screen, and hit play. The screen turned light blue and stayed that way. I pressed FAST FORWARD, advancing through the tape, but the blue screen never changed.

The same was the case with the other two tapes. Either all three were blank—the originals replaced with new—or someone had erased the recorded content.

On the desk, Anna had an old-fashioned rolodex by her phone. I flipped through it until I reached the Z section and found only one contact there: Catherine Zeigler. Marty had given me correct information; Anna's friend lived in Indio, east of Palm Springs, in the low desert outside Los Angeles, a three-hour drive. I removed the card then flipped back through the rolodex until I found the contact info for Paige. His address was in Hancock Park, an upscale community just below Hollywood. I doubted a college kid could afford such digs on his own, even renting, so the house probably belonged to his father.

I called the number for Catherine Zeigler. The call went to voicemail after three rings. Her voice sounded elderly and hesitant on the greeting as she asked me to please leave a message and she'd do her very best to return my call promptly. I didn't leave one. Next, I called the number for the Leary home. No one answered. I committed the address to memory.

Outside, a car honked. The wind picked up and the

house creaked. As I slipped my phone into my pocket, it chirped with an incoming text.

catch me if u can.

I WENT OUT THE WAY I'D COME IN—EXITING THROUGH THE back door, crossing the yard, climbing the hill to Marty and Lenny's property, then cutting across their lawn to my car. I drove past the stationed police car, again turning my head to look the other way, and headed down the lane.

Charley called as I reached the crest of Topanga Canyon and could see the San Fernando Valley below me.

"Sorry about what happened," she said. "Things got messed up. I didn't handle it well. My bad. Forgive me?"

"I'm sorry, as well."

"Let's forget it. We both acted like jerks. It's a tough journey for us, and it's going to take time. Don't ever doubt that I love you. And that I want to marry you."

"That's all I needed to know," I said. "Thank you."

"Don't get mushy. Where are you?"

"On my way to Hancock Park. Then I'm heading home."

"Me too. I'll be there by dinner. See you then."

I wanted to kiss her right through the phone.

15

The Leary house was a Southern-style two-story with walls as white as paper, iron railings, and black shutters that made the place look sinister even in daylight. The place reminded me of something, though I was certain I'd not seen it before. I rang the doorbell. After a bit, a middle-aged black woman in Capri pants and a polo shirt opened the door.

"I'd like to speak with Wyatt Leary, if he's available," I said.

"Mister Wyatt is not here at the moment." The woman had an accent. Maybe Haitian.

"Okay, what about his brother Paige?"

"No one is home right now. I'm sorry. Good day." She went to close the door.

"Well, *you* are," I said, putting a hand on the door and smiling.

"This is not my home, sir, it is my place of employment." Her words were clipped, her diction sharp, and her attitude dismissive. "And since there is no one with whom you can discuss whatever matter you've brought here—"

"I didn't catch your name."

"Angelique Tourneau." It sounded beautiful as it rolled off her tongue.

"Jason Chance." I held out my hand. She took it, shook once, then quickly let go. "And what exactly is it you do for Mr. Leary? If I may ask."

"May *I* ask, why are you here to see Mr. Leary's sons?"

"Official business, a police matter," I said, hoping this might light a fire under her.

Ms. Tourneau sized me up. "Is Mister Wyatt in trouble? Or Mister Paige again?"

"It might be related," I said, though I had no idea to what previous trouble she referred. "Refresh my memory."

She paused before saying, "I was not told details."

"Me either," I said. I leaned toward her, conspiratorially. "They keep us in the dark about everything, don't they? No one seems to realize that without us everything would fall apart. Am I right?"

"Indeed."

"When was this bit of trouble?"

"Several months ago. I was simply asked to contact Mister Adam's attorney to handle an indiscretion. Beyond that, I know nothing."

"Mister Paige's indiscretion?"

She nodded, frowning. I sensed she had little compassion for Mister Paige. It didn't surprise me.

"You never answered my question," I said. "What exactly do you do for Mr. Leary?"

"I take care of his personal affairs. Shall I tell him of your visit?"

"No, thank you," I said, though I knew she most likely would, and I'd probably be hearing soon from his attorney —the one who'd be up my ass like diarrhea. "I'll try to get in touch another time. Goodbye, Ms. Tourneau. By the way, you have a very beautiful name."

"Good day, sir." She closed the door.

So, Paige had some legal troubles in the past. *An indiscretion*, Ms. Tourneau had called it. Something sexual?

As I turned to go, I spotted a white dreamcatcher hanging from the porch eave, dancing in the breeze, and I realized why the house seemed familiar. I stepped down onto the lawn, snapped a few shots of the façade with my phone camera, and texted the pictures to Kathy. She responded immediately: *OMG. That's it. The house in the dream. Where the hell are you?*

WE MET IN BALBOA PARK, BESIDE A SMALL, SERENE LAKE where Kathy had gone to do yoga. I sat on the grass beside her, watching as she scrolled through the various pictures I'd taken of the Leary house.

"Dad, there's no way this is a coincidence." Her voice was alive with excitement. "I've never in my life seen this house outside of these photos right now. Only in that dream I had."

"You're sure?"

"One hundred percent." She handed me back the phone. "What's your logical, rational, natural explanation?" She leaned back, her hands behind her on the yoga mat for support, and gave me a smug look. "Go on, I'll wait."

"Don't be a smartass."

I looked out at the placid waters of the lake, watching three white geese glide across its surface in flawless unison, a perfect triumvirate. One led, the other two kept a slight equidistance behind. Farther on, couples and families were out in paddle boats, moving lazily around the lake with much less grace or precision. Nature can be beautifully synchronized and it can be grossly sloppy. Humans are probably the least graceful on the food chain, and crass—Adam Leary a prime example.

We can also be ridiculously pragmatic and close-minded, even in the face of things beyond our understanding.

"Okay," I said, at last, "let's say you're right, for the sake of argument. What does it mean?"

"It means Paige or Wyatt or Adam Leary had something to do with Janis's murder, and she's pointing me toward one or all of them."

"Isabelle said Paige and Janis were sleeping together. That he took her virginity."

"Janis told me the same thing."

"He's twenty, she was sixteen. No one thought to say anything to anyone?"

Kathy went silent, looking down at her hand as it twisted around blades of grass. Off to the left, a child started to cry. I looked over, saw the little girl sitting on a bench with her mother, sobbing over ice cream that had fallen off the cone to the sidewalk.

"I should have said something to Anna," she finally admitted. "I have no excuse for not doing it." She yanked up a chunk of grass and dirt. "It's hard, when you're a teen yourself, to know how to deal with things like that. Janis was my friend. Not close but getting there. I guess I got scared I might push her away. And there was something about her friendship that made me feel better about myself. Like it was a sign I was getting over my own fucked up trauma. Or maybe it *was* my trauma that kept me from saying anything. Both stupid reasons, I know."

"Not stupid," I said, softening. "We all think we'll make

the right moral choice when faced with one. But thinking it and staring it in the face are two very different things. It's not always easy to know what to do."

"I didn't realize until this moment that I could've maybe saved her life if I'd spoken up."

"We don't know Paige killed her. We don't even know that they slept together. Janis could have made it up."

"Haven't you always told me that the obvious answer is often the right one?"

"But sometimes it isn't."

Kathy leaned over and put her head on my shoulder. "God, I wish life was easier."

"Me too, Katbird," I said, watching the swans take off in flight from the lake and circle over us once before heading off toward the hills.

CARUSO SAT WAITING AT THE SAME TABLE WE'D SHARED before in Tony's Bar and Grill, the same cola drink in front of him, a similar glaze in his eyes. It wasn't yet lunchtime.

"What have you got?" he said. "And it better be good."

"Anna and Billie are in the desert," I said. "Indio, near Palm Springs. With a woman named Catherine Zeigler."

"How'd you come across this info?"

"The how doesn't matter."

"Jesus, you're a pain in the ass." He slurped down some of his drink. "But I appreciate the sharing of info."

"What did you find out about the killing of that teenaged babysitter in Woodland Hills?" I asked.

"MO is similar to Janis Ryker's murder," Caruso said. "The assailant used a knife taken from the kitchen. Left it at the site. No prints. No sign of forced entry. Looks like the girl let the killer in, maybe knew him."

"You have evidence the killer is male?"

"No. But the victim's hands and feet were tied with belts pulled pretty tight, so it was done by somebody strong. And the depth of the stab wounds indicates great force."

"As was the case with Janis."

"I'm not discounting the similarities. It's the only reason I'm sitting here with you now." He nodded a greeting to a pair of uniformed detectives passing by. "So make me a believer."

"I spoke today with a woman who works at the Leary house," I said. "She told me Paige had some trouble with the law a few months ago. She claimed not to know details."

"Okay. That's interesting."

I showed him the most recent texts on my phone. Caruso read aloud. "*I know where they are. Catch me if you can.*"

"I'm wondering if whoever sent these might be trying to bait me," I said. "To make me think he already knows where Billie and Anna are and that they're in danger. Maybe hoping I actually *do* know, and that I'll head there out of concern."

"Leading him to them."

"Yeah."

"And in this playbook of yours, why does he want to find them?"

"He's worried Billie might have seen something. That she may be able to identify him."

"If that's the case, why would she run? Why not just tell us all what she saw?"

"I'm not saying she does know, just that the killer is worried she might."

"Okay. But in his mind, why did she run?"

"She's scared. And her mother's scared. Which blows your theory that Anna's behind the texts, or that Billie is."

"It doesn't blow squat," Caruso said. "Your theory's hypothetical at best."

"Think it through. Anna and Billie would want to keep me as far away from them as possible. Whoever's sending these texts has something else in mind."

"Or they just want you chasing shadows. And they're hoping you can persuade me to follow along." He drank down the rest of his rum and Coke or Jack and Coke or whatever it was he was drinking for breakfast. "You've got to give me more than this."

"Paige Leary made a short film for USC with elements that mimic Janis's murder. Or vice versa. You should have been all over the guy from the beginning."

"Why? I already had my killer."

"Paige was one of Anna's patients, after a DUI arrest. The three videotapes that were out of place in her office coincided with three of his session dates. The tapes were erased or replaced. They're blank now."

"You know this how? Ryker turned them over to you?"

"Yes," I lied.

"Okay, so someone erased tapes that were in Anna Ryker's possession. Anybody could have. Paige Leary wasn't the only patient she recorded on the days in question. It could be completely unrelated. Or maybe she erased them by accident."

"All three?" I said. "Highly unlikely."

"If they're blank, they're useless. They can't prove Paige is guilty. They can't prove he's innocent. That can't do anything. And I still think you're being played."

"Give me twenty-four hours to prove otherwise."

He went quiet, studying me. Finally, he said, "What are you planning to do?"

"Head to Indio."

"You think Leary's going to follow you there and just walk through the door?"

"I believe someone will. Can I ask a favor?"

"It's just one after the other with you, isn't it?" He chuckled. "I'm listening."

"Make contact with Indio PD, get a couple of men to go with me to the Zeigler place."

He clicked his tongue in a steady rhythm as he considered my request. "Okay," he said, at last. "I'll play the hand. But not with locals. Two from LAPD go with you. If you're wrong about this, and I still think you are, at least I'll get something out of it at the end of the day."

By *something*, I knew he meant the arrest of Anna and Billie.

16

Charley had come back home. She stood in the alcove as I walked through the front door. Wordlessly, I went into her arms.

"We're a mess, aren't we?" she whispered.

"I've seen worse," I said.

I kissed her neck, her cheeks, her eyes. Finally, I kissed her delicate, damaged lips. This time, she didn't resist. She took my hand, led me into our bedroom, and closed the door.

It was the first time we'd made love since the fire. In many ways, it was like the first time ever. I was cautious and clumsy, Charley scared and reticent. Like teenagers, afraid of doing something wrong, we had trouble giving ourselves over to each other. Still, it was beautiful, because it meant we were coming back together on every level.

Afterward, lying in bed, Charley nestled in the crook of my arm, her head resting on my shoulder, both of us naked and beaded with sweat, she said, "I want to get married next month."

"I love next month," I said, and kissed the top of her head. "Next is my favorite month of the year."

"Idiot," she said, and snuggled closer.

I closed my eyes, wanting nothing more than to drift off into a blissful, dreamless afternoon sleep with her, though I know I couldn't. Charley sat up, pulling away from me. She took some cream from the nightstand and rubbed it on her neck and shoulder.

"You're in pain," I said. "I'm sorry."

"It was worth it." She took my hand, looked into my eyes, and smiled.

I paused, then said, "I've got to go."

"Where?"

"I'm heading to the desert." I told her about the texts and my last meeting with Caruso. "I want to check on Anna and Billie, and I may be able to lure whoever sent those texts and threatened them out into the open." I got up and pulled on my jeans. From the closet, I took down an overnight bag.

"How long do you think you'll be gone?"

"Probably overnight."

"Okay," she said, flatly.

I glanced down at her. She stared at the ceiling. After a bit, she said, "Do you think she's got a crush on you?"

"Who?"

"Doctor Ryker."

"Anna?" The query surprised me.

"Yes, *Anna*. I'm curious, is all."

"No, I don't," I said. "She thinks I believe her daughter is a killer." I removed clothes from the bureau and put them into the bag. "She told me she was sorry she ever brought me into this situation."

"How close are the two of you? You met her before you and I got back together. Be honest."

"Is this a genuine question? Right after we've made love?"

"It's a genuine question right after you told me you were heading off to spend the night with her right."

"I'm not spending the night with her. I'm trying to catch a killer." I stopped packing and sat on the edge of the bed, putting a hand on her calf. Her skin and muscles tensed at my touch. "Anna and I are friends. She's helped Kathy with her recovery. And she's talked me off a few ledges. You know all that."

"Whenever she calls, you don't hesitate to answer."

"I'm working a case that's deeply traumatic for her."

"And now you're driving off to the desert to follow a lead that probably came from Billie."

"You think that, as well?"

She paused. "I don't know what I think." She rolled on her side to face me. "You've never thought about her, romantically? Tell me the truth. I won't get mad."

"No. Never."

"Not once? A little? When you first met? She's a smart, beautiful woman."

"I seriously don't want to have this conversation, Charley. It makes no sense."

"Love is illogical."

"Well, as illogical as it may seem, I love you and only you."

"Scars and all?"

"Your injuries don't matter to me. And they don't define you."

"But they're always going to be here. They won't ever go away. Not completely. And I'm scared I'll always be wondering, why did he stay? Why did he stick it out? Guilt? Pity? Fear of looking like an asshole for walking away?"

"That's a fucked-up way of thinking," I blurted, then caught myself. "I'm sorry. That was a bad response."

"Yeah, it was." She frowned. "Forget it. I'm being stupid. Acting like a jealous teenager. The poor woman is terrified, going through hell, and all I can worry about is if she wants to sleep with you. I can't seem to get anything right anymore."

"Don't say that. You're trying. And I'm glad you see how ridiculous the notion sounds." Again, not the best choice of words.

"We should probably stop talking before things go off the rails," she said.

"Charley ..."

"I'm tired. I need to rest. Have a safe trip." She turned away from me.

Two steps forward, one step back.

I HEADED FOR INDIO. THE CONVERSATION (*ARGUMENT, FIGHT*) with Charley haunted me the entire drive. I didn't believe she really felt jealousy toward Anna. Anna was just an easy target for the insecurities Charley's injuries had ignited. And as smart as I liked to believe I was, I still hadn't figured out the best way to maneuver these rough waters.

As I inched along in the afternoon traffic, trying to get out of Los Angeles, I had an urge to duck into a dark, cool bar and calm my nerves with a blast or two of bourbon. Alcohol was the escape-drug-of-choice for many my age, second maybe only to marijuana (and a close second, at that). For the young—teens like Billie and Wyatt and Janis —the drug seemed to be the Internet. Equally addictive. Maybe not physically as damaging, but psychologically, perhaps worse. A cyber realm that brought the world closer together yet made everyone feel lonely and ostracized.

Like Janis. Like Billie.

I didn't stop for the drink. Traffic sped up, and soon the green rolling peaks and deep valleys of the San Gabriel mountains gave way to the rocky, arid brown terrain of the Coachella Valley. I got to Indio by four-thirty, half an hour behind schedule.

Catherine Zeigler's house—a contemporary Spanish with terra-cotta roof, large windows, and walls the color of the desert sand that surrounded it—was the last home on a single-block road called Gaviota that ended at a fenced-in open field. The low sun to the west was strong in my eyes as I approached, the air dry and hot. A moderate wind lifted up sand and grit that felt prickly on my skin.

A male and a female in plainclothes sat in a nondescript sedan half a block from the house: Caruso's officers, in place and ready. Their car windows were down. Each had a large cup of coffee in hand. Sweat beaded on their brows. As I passed them, the female driver gave me a slight nod.

Anna's red Volvo was parked in the driveway of Catherine's home, behind a much newer white Mercedes SUV. The sedan had a thin layer of dust across its metal and glass—it had been sitting there for some time. Wiper marks showed on the SUV; it had recently been driven.

The curtains were pulled shut across the front bay window of the house. White plastic Venetian blinds were closed on the second-floor windows. This made the house look guarded and secretive. A walkway of stone weaved through desert blooms to a small portico and a large front door, painted red. I pushed a doorbell button. Inside, I heard a two-tone chime, then nothing else. No voices. No sound of movement.

I stepped to the bay window and peered in through a sliver of space between the curtains but saw only the corner of a dark living room. I took out my cell and called Catherine Zeigler's house phone, reading the number off the card I'd taken from Anna's office. I heard the ring from inside. Catherine's elderly, genteel voice on the answering machine asked me to leave a message.

"This is Jason Chance, Ms. Zeigler," I said. "I'm outside your house. I need to speak with Anna Ryker. I know she's here. Please let me in."

I ended the call and waited. No one came to the door. As I stepped back onto the front lawn to look up at the second-floor windows, my cell buzzed. Caruso calling.

"Where are you?" he asked.

"Outside the Zeigler place. Your officers are down the street."

"That's Margie Zeravsky and Jeff Steen. They have orders to give you some leeway but not a whole lot."

"Comforting," I said.

"Anybody home?"

"Yes, but no one's answering the door. Is there a purpose to this call, or are you just checking up on me?"

"I thought you'd want to know, I got that info on Paige Leary," Caruso said. "Six months ago, he was charged with sexually assaulting a sixteen-year-old girl. The charges were dropped a month later by the victim's family, and the DA went along with the decision. Why, I have no idea. She subsequently claimed she was just pissed at Paige because he didn't call her after they'd gone out on a date, so she made up the rape thing to punish him. Three weeks later, the girl had a major role on Adam Leary's TV show."

"He got her to drop a rape charge by offering her a part?"

"Fucking Hollywood, huh?"

"What were the details of the attack?"

"In the initial report, the girl claimed Paige held a kitchen knife to her throat and forced her into his bedroom. In her recant, she said she made it all up."

"No rape kit was done?"

"Nope. The family didn't even report it for three days."

"Did the DA go after her for false charges after she recanted?"

"No. I guess he didn't feel it was worth it. Liars tend to hurt the credibility of real victims when they try to come forward."

"Except she wasn't lying. She'd been bought off."

"Who knows? Maybe Papa Leary got to the assistant DA handling the case, as well."

"You ready to believe there's something to this?" I asked.

"We'll see. Nobody got murdered six months ago, the victim just got famous. That's a long way from what happened to the Ryker girl."

"I'll keep you posted on what goes down here."

"You better," Caruso said. "You have three hours until those officers arrest Billie and Anna Ryker. That's clear, right?"

"Like water," I said.

I rang the front bell one last time. No one came to the door. The side gate was locked but low enough to jump over. I walked along a dog run and into a backyard filled with high-end patio furniture, a built-in barbecue station, a large pool, and a waterfall cascading down a rock wall into a small jacuzzi. The retractable awning attached to the side of the house gave shade to a patio table and six chairs outside a sliding glass door that blazed with reflected sunlight. I cupped my hands and peered into an open kitchen and adjoining den. A widescreen TV was tuned to a golf game, but there was no one watching. Steam rose up from a tea kettle on the stove.

    I rapped on the glass. No one came, so I tried the door. It was unlocked and easily slid open with a greased metal-on-metal sound, like someone saying, *"Ssshhhh."* A blast of cool air enveloped me as I stepped inside, and I caught a whiff of the overwhelming and unmistakable stench of death.

PART II

"BURIED ALIVE IN THE BLUES"

17

Catherine Zeigler's body lay face down in a corridor that fed off the back den—eyes open, no pulse, blood from a gaping neck wound congealing on the polished marble floor. I phoned Officer Zeravsky.

"I'm inside the house," I told her. "One dead body, so far. I'm assuming it's Catherine Zeigler."

"Stay where you are," she said. "Don't touch anything. We're on our way." She spoke as if reprimanding some neighbor who'd blundered into a crime scene.

"I'll unlock the front door for you," I said, and ended the call.

I left Catherine's body, Beretta in hand, and headed for the front of the house, entering a living room of simple furniture, unspectacular modern artwork, and vaulted ceilings the height of the house. To my left, a round archway led to a grand foyer with a semi-circular staircase to the second floor. The steps were polished hardwood with a crimson-colored runner. I walked over to the front door, unlocked it, and pulled it ajar. Then, not waiting for Steen and Zeravsky, I went upstairs, praying I'd find Billie and Anna alive.

The bedrooms were on the east side of the house: four doors, two on each side of a narrow corridor. All were closed. The first, a master bedroom I assumed belonged to Catherine, had a lived-in feel; the bureau top was covered with perfume bottles, a vanity near the window was littered with makeup and nail polish bottles. The bed was made, its floral duvet smooth and tight. A jacket and pair of pants had been carefully draped across a mustard-colored chaise lounge. I looked in the master bathroom, saw nothing of merit, so left the bedroom and moved on.

The next door opened into a smaller chamber, pink and white, childish and feminine. The woman downstairs looked to be in her late fifties or early sixties, so I wondered if she had a grown daughter who'd been raised here but had moved out, off to college or just life away from Mom. Perhaps this was the room in which Billie stayed—though there were no signs of a visiting guest: no suitcase or backpack out in the open, no clothes in evidence, save a pair of small jeans balled up under a corner chair.

Officer Zeravsky called out my name downstairs. I crossed to the bedroom door. "I'm up here," I said. "The body is in the back corridor."

"What are you doing?" Steen said.

"We told you to stay put," Zeravsky said.

"Relax, it's not my first crime scene. We do need to contact the locals soon, though."

I headed for the third door in the hallway. It opened to yet another bedroom, this one as dark as night, with thick curtains pulled across the window and the lights turned off. I felt along the side wall, searching for the light switch. When I found it and flipped it up, lamps on each of the nightstands came to life, casting a soft amber glow throughout the room.

Anna was face-up on the bed, her eyes closed. A large kitchen knife protruded from her upper abdomen, just below the sternum. I hurried to her side and lifted an arm, feeling for a pulse on her wrist.

She was still alive.

Four Indio PD officers arrived off a call from Steen, along with an ambulance and two paramedics. A homicide detective from the IPD showed up soon after, along with the local coroner and his team. The detective—a man named Rooney who looked to be in his early 60s, but with the energy and intensity of someone half that age—questioned Zeravsky, Steen, and me.

"How'd you discover the body and the other victim?" Rooney asked me. "Who let you into the house?" He worked to sound tough, in charge.

"I smelled the decomposition from the porch," I said, stretching the truth. "I've worked a lot of homicides. It's an unmistakable odor. The front door was locked, so we went around to the back. The patio door was open. We entered and identified ourselves, then followed the smell and found the first victim."

Steen and Zeravsky didn't contradict my inclusion of them in the initial search. They didn't want things to snag over a technicality any more than I did. They'd come here to arrest two people. None of us anticipated the turn the situation had taken. I'm sure they wanted to keep a rein on things as much as I did, despite local jurisdiction.

"You should have called us first," he said.

"If we'd waited," Zeravsky said, "it's possible Ms. Ryker would not still be alive."

Rooney nodded. "So, you're LAPD, huh?" I caught a hint of longing in his voice and eyes.

"I'm an ex-cop," I told him. "The sheriff's department. I was hired by one of today's victims." I gave a bare bones sketch of the case.

Before Rooney could comment, the coroner approached and filled him in on Anna's condition. The stab wound was deep. It had caused a great deal of blood loss. We would not know the extent of any internal damage until she got to the hospital.

I watched with concern as the coroner's team wheeled Anna out of the house on a gurney and loaded her into the back of the ambulance that would take her to nearby John F. Kennedy Memorial Hospital. Two thoughts ran simultaneously through my head: *Don't die, Anna* and *where is Billie?*

The local first responders brought over a neighbor to identify the body in the hallway. Horrified by the sight and smell of the corpse, the elderly man quickly confirmed that the woman was, indeed, Catherine Zeigler. He then hurried back outside, looking pale and shaky as he held a hand over his mouth and started to weep.

"I've known her since she first moved to the desert," he told us. "Ten years now. She was a good soul. Always took time to say hello and ask how I was doing. This kind of thing shouldn't happen to a person like that. And not in a place like this. What a world."

As an officer led him back to his home, he faltered on the sidewalk and would have fallen to his knees had the policeman not grabbed his arm to support him.

"No sign of the daughter?" Rooney asked.

Steen and Zeravsky shook their heads.

"Either she's our perp, or she's been abducted by whoever did this," Rooney said. He barked out orders, dispatching men to search the house and grounds for Anna's daughter. The case seemed to have galvanized him. A small town like Indio probably had a low murder rate, so this was a big deal for Rooney. And I suppose he smelled opportunity. *Local Detective Helps Los Angeles Police Crack Big City Murder Investigation.*

What *had* happened here? Was it possible Billie killed Catherine Zeigler, stabbed her own mother, and ran? Or had she been taken hostage, as Rooney suggested? If so, by whom? Was this the work of Paige Leary? How had he gotten here first? Had I been wrong in thinking *I* was leading *him*?

Stepping outside, I called Caruso and filled him in. "If Billie is involved," I said, "and I still think that's a big *if*, then I doubt she's working alone. Or whoever did this may have taken her by force. I'm going to the hospital to check on Anna, find out what I can from her."

"Okay by me," Caruso said. "Zeravsky and Steen will search the neighborhood, look for the kid. Make no mistake, if they find her, they're bringing her back to LA. And the locals will put a guard on Anna's door."

"Good. She might still be a target." I ended the call. Detective Rooney was just coming out of the house. "Any sign of Billie Ryker?" I asked him.

He shook his head. "You got any other suspects?"

"Nothing worth mentioning," I said.

He sipped some coffee from a takeout paper cup. "Coroner said the assailant came up behind Catherine Zeigler," he said, "and slashed her throat, right to left. Means he was probably left-handed."

I tried to remember if I'd seen Paige favor his left hand

with any actions when we'd met. From what I could recall, he'd used both.

"And whoever stabbed Anna was looking down at her when it happened," Rooney added. "If she was conscious, she could have seen his face."

"I'd like to speak with her as soon as she's capable of answering questions."

"I imagine that won't be until tomorrow morning. And I get first dibs. My city, my murder."

"Understood," I said.

I asked for a good local motel. He gave me the name of one, then handed me his card with his contact info.

"What a mess," he said, heading to his car. He didn't sound disturbed. He was excited.

A local cruiser was still parked across the street, facing the Zeigler house, with two officers inside. The crime scene unit would be here at least another hour. I walked down to my car and got behind the wheel, made a U-turn, and drove down Gaviota. There I turned right, then made another right on Tortuga. This street also dead-ended at the open field. I parked, turned off the engine, and waited.

18

Once darkness came, I jumped the chain link fence to the field and followed it back toward the Zeigler place. A cinderblock retaining wall like the one I'd repaired at home separated the house from the open lot. I hoisted myself up and over it, and dropped down into the Zeigler backyard.

The smell of death inside the empty and quiet home had lessened with the removal of the body, but a trace of it still hung in the air. The puddle of congealed blood remained in the corridor where Catherine Zeigler had fallen. Investigators never clean the physical mess left by murder, they only study it. An outside service would come in once the crime scene was released from investigation. Until then, the interior would remain untouched, like a macabre exhibit in a museum, giving the detectives the opportunity to return and re-walk the scene as needed. To look for new clues and see the crime from a different perspective.

My first concern was not to solve the murder, though; it

was to find Billie, or at least something that would lead me to her.

I went upstairs, back to the bedroom I'd assumed she'd used. I searched the drawers of the bureau and the medicine cabinet in the bathroom. In the closet, I found a couple of cardboard boxes. One contained folded sweaters, winter coats, gloves, caps, and scarves. The other was filled with paperback books, some teen magazines, a few pads of lined white paper filled with neat handwriting—someone's homework—and a small jewelry box. A tiny dancer sprung up as I opened the box's lid, and it spun on a small disk while *The Waltz of the Flowers* from Tchaikovsky's *The Nutcracker* ballet played. In its little holding compartment were two small rings on a thin silver chain, a necklace of green and yellow beads like the ones used during Mardi Gras in New Orleans, a small brooch of ruby-colored stones in the shape of a butterfly, and a crudely made clay statuette of a bird with the name *Janis* etched into the bottom. It was the statue Anna told us had gone missing from her office. Did Billie bring it? Or had it been planted, to make us think she did?

I knew what Caruso would think.

I slipped the statue into my pocket and kept searching. Billie had shoved her carryon suitcase under the bed. It was zipped up tight, with her clothes neatly folded inside. She'd kept it ready to go at a moment's notice. If she'd willingly left with whoever had come and attacked Anna and Catherine Zeigler, she would have taken the suitcase with her. That she hadn't troubled me.

In the bedroom where I'd found Anna, a suitcase lay open on the floor by the window. This one felt lived out of, not prepped to flee. I crouched down and searched through the contents: jeans, shirts, underwear, and a couple of pairs of shoes filled the main compartment. In one of the bag's side pockets, I found items I knew belonged to Janis, tangible memories Anna must have taken from her dead daughter's bedroom before going on the run: a jade necklace with matching earrings, a small stuffed rabbit, a collection of photos.

Elements of sadness and ones of suspicion in both rooms, but no sign of Billie or clues to her whereabouts.

"We got a hit on one of the fingerprints from the kitchen knife," Rooney told me over the phone.

"You've got to be kidding," I said. "How the hell did you make that happen so fast?"

"It's not the process that takes time," he said, "it's the backlog. You know that. Our lab isn't overloaded the way I imagine it is in LA. Our technician was excited to have something to work on and got right to it. A print came back with a hit, thanks to your LA case. Belongs to your victim's sister, Billie Ryker."

Another brick in the wall.

I could already hear Caruso, gloating: *Give it up, Chance, we got her. The knife that killed Catherine Zeigler, and was used to stab Anna Ryker, with Billie's prints all over it ... Billie's condition the night of the murder and her admission of some sort of guilt ... Anna and Billie's flight from Los Angeles ... The argument between Billie and Janis ... No sign of forced entry in either home ... The texts from Janis's missing phone ... Janis's clay statue in the Indio house ... Game over, man. It's a slam dunk. Two counts of murder and one attempted.*

Yet it still felt wrong to me. Too easy to connect the dots. There was more at work here. Another level in play. And I could not shake the feeling Paige Leary was involved. Had he bested me? Somehow been one step ahead the whole time? I'd come here thinking I was leading the killer into a trap. Now, it seemed, I'd been led. The killer wanted me to find another body, with more evidence condemning Billie. I'd been duped. Tricked by texts I didn't understand.

That, or Billie really was the killer.

If so, who sent me the texts? And why?

I went out into the backyard. The sky above me was as black as a deep abyss, not a star to be seen. I put my hands in my pocket and stood on the lawn, staring up into space like a child waiting to see a UFO. My palm wrapped around the crude bird statue. Touching it, I felt a sudden dizziness come on, an unbalanced sense that coursed through my body. I closed my eyes and leaned forward, putting my hands on my knees, and took a few deep breaths. I didn't feel nauseous. The sensation was closer to a rush of adrenaline. Eventually the dizziness passed, and my legs found their strength again. As I straightened up, I glanced at the back wall of the garage—the one place in the house I'd not looked.

Its exterior side door was unlocked. I stepped inside and flipped a wall switch. A single exposed bulb in a ceiling socket came to life, shining down on an old station wagon in the middle of the garage. It was partially covered by a dust-coated tarp, though in several spots the dust had been smudged by handprints. The floor of the garage had a coating of dust, as well. Two pairs of feet had recently stomped through—most likely Rooney's team. They'd rounded the car, lifted the tarp and found nothing, walked to the side door from which I'd entered, and returned to the house. It took a moment for me to spot a third set of footprints, smaller in size and lighter in imprint.

The steps of a child.

A bump in the tarp on the left side of the car indicated the passenger door had not been completely closed by the officers. I walked over, threw the tarp up, grabbed the door handle, and pulled. The hinges creaked from lack of use as the door opened. No interior lights came on. Blankets and stacks of old, yellowing newspapers littered the rear seat, creating a mound in the center. The car stank of mildew and age. I was about to close the door again when something caught my eye. The edge of a small, black-and-white Converse sneaker peeked out of the far corner of the mound.

I pushed the fabric and papers aside, and there she was, curled in a frightened ball, arms wrapped tightly around her knees, pulling them against her chest. She seemed to be holding her breath in terror.

"Billie? It's okay," I said. "It's me, Jason Chance. You don't have to be afraid. Come out."

19

Her hair was matted with perspiration, the jet-black bangs clinging to her pale forehead. Her arms glistened with a slick film. Sweat stained the collar of her red and black T-shirt. God knows how long she'd been hiding under the heavy blankets and stacks of newspaper. The windows of the car were up, and the garage was not air conditioned. That she hadn't passed out astonished me.

"Let's get you out of this hot car and inside," I said. "You'll need some water."

Billie took my hand and let me pull her across the seat and out of the car, the newspaper and blankets crinkling and rumpling in her wake. As we walked to the garage door and into the house, she never let go her hold.

"Where's my mom?" she asked, her voice weak and cracking.

"We'll talk about her in a minute. We need to go inside where it's cool."

In the kitchen, I filled a glass with water from the tap,

added ice from the dispenser in the freezer door, and handed it to her. She drank thirstily, holding the glass in both hands, her arms trembling.

"How long were you out there?" I asked.

"Since the man came."

"What man? Do you know his name?"

"No." She wiped her lips with her forearm. "Mom just told me he wanted to hurt us and that I had to hide."

"Did she tell you why?"

"He thinks I know what happened to Janis. That's why we had to run away from LA." She looked around, scared, as though the threat might return. "Where's my mom? I want to see her. She's okay, right?"

"She's at the hospital. Whoever came to the house did hurt her. But she's alive. We can visit her soon."

She swayed and sat on one of the kitchen table chairs. "I'm tired. My head hurts."

"When was the last time you ate something?"

She didn't answer. I stood and crossed to the fridge, took out a packet of bread, a jar of peanut butter, and one of jelly. "PB and J all right?" She nodded. I took out two slices of bread, spreading jam on one and peanut butter on the other. I put the sandwich on a napkin and placed it in front of her. Billie grabbed it up and took a large bite.

"How did you know to go hide in the car?" I asked.

"Mom sent me to the garage. She seemed really scared."

I wondered, had someone already come into the house when Anna told Billie to hide? Why hadn't she gone with her daughter? Had she thought she could fend off the attacker?

"You're sure you didn't get a glimpse of the man? The intruder."

"No. I never saw him. I just did what Mom said. I got into the car and covered myself with the blankets and newspapers. It stunk awful in there, and it was so hot. But she made me promise not to come out again until she came and got me." Billie's eyes teared up. "She never did." She cried then, soft, quivering breaths mixed with moans.

"Who else knows you came here to Indio? I need you to be completely open with me. Your life, and your mom's, depends on it. Who, besides Marty and Lenny, knows you're here?"

"Wyatt," she muttered.

"Wyatt Leary?"

She nodded.

"When was the last time you spoke with him?"

"Last night. After we got here. I called him. He said he was going to come get me. We were going to run away together."

"You gave him the address?"

"Yeah."

"Did he mention Paige?"

"No. Why would he?"

"You knew Janis and Paige had a relationship, right?"

She pushed the sandwich away. "I want to see my mom."

"It's too late tonight. We can go see her in morning."

"No!" she said, slamming her palm on the tabletop. "I want to see her now!" A childish, bratty anger had come over her. She knocked the water glass to the floor. "Take me to her or I'll break everything in this room."

I understood the fear driving her outburst, and I sympathized. She needed to know her mother was alive. How could I not give her that? I considered calling Detective Rooney so he could clear the way at the hospital, but then he'd want to question Billie. Subjecting her to a police interrogation now would more than likely push her to shut down again.

"Okay," I said. "Let's go try."

It was almost nine when we arrived at the hospital. A young woman in light blue scrubs looked up from the computer screen she'd been studying as I approached the reception desk with Billie.

"May I help you?" she said.

"I'm detective Jason Chance, with the LA Sheriff's Department." I saw no way around the lie this time. I hoped the assertiveness in my voice supplanted the need to flash a badge. "It's imperative I see a patient. Anna Ryker. She's the knife wound victim brought in earlier this evening."

The nurse looked at me then Billie, who fidgeted, shifting from one foot to the other while staring at the floor. "I'd have to okay it with the doctor," the nurse said. "Normally no one is allowed to visit until 9:00 a.m."

"I understand that's policy," I said. "But this is her daughter, Billie. She hasn't seen her mother since the incident that put Ms. Ryker here. The young girl is on the verge of a panic attack and needs to know her mom is okay. Five minutes, that's all we need. Ms. Ryker should be out of both surgery and recovery by now. Please."

"It's okay, Mary." The voice came from off to my left. I turned and saw a uniformed officer approaching with a paper cup of coffee in his hand. I recognized him as one of the IPD cops who'd first arrived at Catherine Zeigler's house, the one who'd brought the neighbor over to identify the body. "He's from Los Angeles. Part of a bigger investigation, apparently."

I looked at the officer and nodded in gratitude. He said, "Does Detective Rooney know you found the kid?"

"I just spoke with him," I said, hoping he wouldn't check.

The woman typed something on the computer keyboard in front of her. "Ms. Ryker's out of post-op. Second floor. Room two-zero-five."

"Come on," the officer said. "I'll show you."

Relieved, I put a hand on Billie's shoulder and guided her around the nurse's station. We followed the officer into an elevator car on the other side of the reception area. "How's she doing?" I asked.

"Couldn't tell you. I just came on duty. Anyway, I leave the medical stuff to the pros and hope they do the same with us. Know what I mean?" He stared at Billie as if he wanted to say something to her yet couldn't find the correct words.

Billie squeezed my hand as we rode up to the second floor and walked down its quiet hallway. A second officer sat in a plastic chair outside room 205, reading something on an iPad. He looked up as we approached.

"Hey, Grant," he said to the officer who'd brought us. "What's going on?"

"This is that private detective from Los Angeles. The girl needs to see that her mom's okay. I told them it was cool. Five minutes."

The second officer gave me the once-over before nodding and standing. "You clear it with Rooney?"

"He did." Officer Grant cocked a thumb in my direction.

"Then I guess I'm outta here. Have a good one." He headed for the elevator.

Grant motioned toward the hospital door. I eased it open and let Billie go into the room before me. Anna lay on her back in bed, eyes closed, nasal prongs for oxygen in her nostrils and an IV in her arm. A monitor behind her *beeped* softly. The other two beds were partially obscured by division curtains but appeared to be empty. I could see the bulge of a bandage on Anna's abdomen, under her hospital gown.

Billie turned to me and put her arms around my waist, pressing her forehead against my side. "Why won't she open her eyes?" she whispered.

"She was hurt pretty badly," I said. "They had to give her strong medicine that helps ease the pain. She might not even know we're here. But see those machines? They monitor her heart, her blood pressure, and other things. They show that she's doing all right."

"Billie," Anna said, her voice barely audible. She turned toward us, opening her eyes.

"Mom!" Billie ran to Anna's side.

"Careful," I warned. "She's still weak and injured."

"It's okay," Anna said. "I don't care." She put her untethered arm around her daughter's shoulder and pulled her close. Billie buried her head in the sheets that covered her mother's legs.

"She demanded I bring her," I said. "She's a strong-willed young woman." Anna nodded. "How do you feel?" I asked.

"Numb from the chest down. Groggy." Struggling to speak, she asked, "Cathy okay?"

I shook my head.

Tears welled in Anna's eyes. She pulled her daughter closer.

"He found me in the car," Billie said, her voice muffled by the sheets. "I was so scared, Mom, when you didn't come."

"I know, sweetie. I'm sorry." She looked up at me. "How did you find me?"

"Marty."

"I figured he'd crack."

"Don't blame him. I was relentless." I stepped closer to the bed. "We don't have a lot of time, Anna. Detective Caruso's men are going to arrest you the minute you're well enough to leave here. Billie, too, I'm afraid. I need to know what happened. Who got in the house? Who attacked you?"

"I don't know," Anna said. "I never saw his face. He wore a mask."

"Any sense who it could have been?"

"No. He was tall. And strong. It happened so fast." She swallowed. Even this action seemed painful for her.

"How did you know he was there? What prompted you to send Billie to the garage?"

"I heard the patio door slide open. I'd just sat down to meditate in a study by the kitchen. Billie was in her room. Catherine had gone to the store. The house was very quiet and I heard that sliding noise." She tried to replicate the sound. "I knew something was wrong. I *knew*. There are back stairs to the second floor. I hurried up. Told Billie to go out to the garage. To the old car there. '*Hide*,' I said." She closed her eyes, inhaled slowly, then exhaled. The retelling was a struggle for her.

"Why didn't you go with her?" I asked.

"I needed to call the police."

"But you didn't."

"Never got the chance. I heard the struggle in the hallway. Catherine had come home while I spoke to Billie. I went to the top of the stairs. And I saw him step into the foyer. All in black. Wearing a plastic mask. White, with no details, like they sell at Halloween. There was a knife in his hand. Bloody. He bounded up the stairs and chased me into the bedroom. He was so fast. So strong. He knocked me over. Took the phone out of my hand before I could call. That's the last thing I remember."

"It was Wyatt's father," Billie blurted out, looking up at me. "*He* did it. He attacked my mom. Killed Mrs. Zeigler. And *he* killed Janis. It was Adam Leary."

20

Billie's admission caught me off guard. "Why would you think it was Adam Leary?" I said.

"Wyatt told me."

"Honey, I think Wyatt's confused," Anna said.

"No. He knows. I believe him."

"Why would Wyatt think this?" I said.

"Some phone call he heard," Billie said. "He didn't give me details. We didn't have a lot of time when we spoke."

Adam Leary? Not Paige? Why? What motive?

And if Wyatt believed his father had killed Janis, why allow the police to arrest Billie? Why let her mom turn her into a fugitive?

"Why did Wyatt keep his suspicions from the police?" I asked. "Why did he tell only you?"

"Because there's no proof. He didn't think the police would believe him."

"If there's no proof, why does *he* believe it?"

"I don't know. You'll have to ask him."

"Where is he?"

"I don't know that either."

"When did he tell you all this?"

"Last night, when I called him."

"I'm having trouble buying it," Anna said. "I treated Paige. In the sessions, he talked a lot about his father. Painted a strong picture of the man. Selfish, yes. Cold. Loose in his parenting. But nothing to give me any indication he was capable of something so brutal and horrid."

"Wyatt says we're all capable of things we don't expect we are," Billie said, "under the right circumstances."

"Look at my session tapes," Anna said to me. "I give you permission. Maybe there's something there I don't remember or didn't catch. Or that means something in this new light. Take them from my office—"

"I've already looked at them," I said. "They were blank. Either erased or replaced. I'm guessing there was something damning on them. Or whoever erased or replaced them feared there was."

The door opened behind me and a short man in a white coat stepped in. "What's going on, here?"

"I'm Sheriff's Detective Jason Chance from Los Angeles," I said. "This is Billie Ryker. She needed to see her mother. And I needed to ask Ms. Ryker a few questions about her attack."

"I don't care who you are," the doctor said. "You must leave right now."

"I don't want to go," Billie said, looking up at Anna.

"It's okay, honey," Anna said. "I have to rest. As do you. You can come back first thing in the morning. I'll be stronger then."

"Mom, please. Let me stay. I'll sleep in that chair. Or on the floor."

"I'm sorry, that's out of the question," the doctor said.

"You can come back in a few hours," Anna said. "Promise." She hugged her daughter again, holding on like she feared it was the last time.

THE WIND WAS STRONG AS WE WALKED ACROSS THE NEARLY empty hospital parking lot, the swirling sand creating a fog-like opaqueness that muted the overhead street lamps and made it difficult to see more than a few feet.

"Is my mom going to die?" Billie said.

"No. They're taking good care of her." I had no idea if this was true, but how could I frighten the girl any more than she already was?

She climbed into the passenger seat of my Jeep and slammed shut the door. We drove to a motel three blocks from the hospital. The elderly woman who checked us in assumed Billie was my daughter, and I didn't dissuade her of the notion. Inside, Billie immediately headed for the bathroom, closing the door. I tried to call Charley. She didn't pick up. I phoned Kathy.

"I'm still in Indio," I told her. "How's Charley?"

"Acting weird," Kathy said. "She's been in the bedroom most of the day. She only came out to get coffee and some food. When I asked her what was wrong, she shrugged and said only that she was having a down day and not to worry about it."

"Okay," I said.

"Did you two have a fight or something?"

"It's all just overwhelming for her. Like you told me, we need to give her space."

"Yeah." Kathy paused. "What's happening in Indio?"

"I'll fill you in when I get back. Which probably won't be

until tomorrow afternoon."

"Are Billie and Doctor Ryker okay?"

"They will be. We'll talk tomorrow. I love you. And tell Charley I love her, too. And that I'm sorry."

"Sorry for what? Dad, what did you do?"

"Nothing. Everything. She'll understand. Goodnight." I ended the call.

Billie came out of the bathroom. She'd taken a quick shower and put her clothes back on.

"I feel yucky in these, but my clothes are all still back at the house," she said.

"We'll get them in the morning," I said.

She sat on the edge of one of the beds. Her eye twitched. I took the clay bird statue from my jacket pocket.

"How did this get into the closet in your room at Catherine Zeigler's house?" I asked. "Did you put it there?"

She looked at it, curiously. "Is that mine or Janis's?" I turned it over to show her Janis's name scrawled across the bottom. "That's supposed to be in my mom's office. She's had it there for years. Since we made them."

"Someone took it. And it ended up here in Indio."

"It wasn't me. Why would I?"

"A keepsake. A memory."

"I don't like memories." Thirteen years old and she'd already grown jaded about the past. I couldn't help thinking in that moment that the world moves too fast. "Ever heard that song by Ataris, 'The Boys of Summer'?" she said. "*Never look back*."

"Don Henley sang it first," I said. "But I get your point."

She held her hand out for the statue. "Can I?"

I handed it to her. She looked at the artifact with sadness. "This one's better than mine. Janis's artwork always was." She set the bird down on the bed. "He put it in that closet for you to find. He must really want to hurt me."

"You're an easy target."

"Why?"

I paused. "You really don't remember anything about the night your sister was killed?" Billie shrugged; it was neither a denial or acknowledgement. "You found her body. Marty Astor discovered you wandering Horseshoe Lane, covered in blood, with the murder weapon in your hand." It was a cruel image to slam her with, if indeed she didn't remember. If she was guilty, it didn't matter. But if she was being framed, she needed to know the method. "Why were you out there? Why did Marty find you that way?"

"I don't remember!" She scooted back on the bed, pulling her knees to her chest and wrapping her arms around them. "I just want her back," she said, and teared up. "I don't want her to be dead."

"I know, Billie. It's hard to lose the people you love."

"Are you going to let them arrest me?"

"You already have been arrested, Billie," I said. "A judge let you go home in your mom's care. But charges against you have already been filed. Those charges will only be dropped if we find rock-solid evidence against someone else. Maybe that's Adam Leary. But I've got to have proof. Talk to me about Wyatt. You and he are close, aren't you?"

"We're in love."

"Isn't he a little old for you?"

"Four years is not that much. He's still a teenager."

"Did he come see you at Catherine Zeigler's house?"

"Yes," she said, looking down at her hands. "I mean, he tried to. I told him when I called him that I wanted him to come get me."

"When did he arrive?"

"I don't know. Mom got to me and sent me to hide before he showed up. I never saw him. Then everything went to hell."

Now I knew why. The killer followed Wyatt, not me.

"Where is Wyatt now?" I asked.

"I don't know. I guess back in LA." She leaned against the headboard and closed her eyes. I could tell her mind was already starting to shut down. She had given me all she could tonight.

"We should try and get some sleep," I said. I stepped over to the door and bolted it shut. "Can I trust you not to run?"

"Where am I going to go? I've got nowhere now."

I reached over and shut off the lamp on the stand. Amber light from the parking lot, muted by the diaphanous curtains, lit the room, along with an occasional red flare from the neon motel sign blinking on and off. I sat in a chair and watched Billie. Her eyes remained closed, and her lips were moving. Perhaps she was praying. Maybe talking to herself, trying to calm down. Or quietly singing the lyrics to a song she found comforting. I'd done that myself, in times of stress.

Despite everything I'd learned in the last several days, the case had grown more confusing. Two vicious murders (with a third attempted) didn't seem like Adam Leary's style; he was the kind of Hollywood scum that used money and power to cover up crimes, not brute force. But, then again, who knows? Maybe a situation had arisen beyond that scope. Paige raped a sixteen-year-old and Leary made the accusation disappear. Had Paige raped Janis, too? Did Adam Leary try the same tactic on her, offering a role on his TV show to shut her up? If Janis refused and threatened to tell her mom and the police, it would have pushed the Learys into a corner. *Desperate people do desperate things.* Was Adam the kind of man who would kill to protect his son? Given the sexual abuse charges *he* faced, had the pressure of it all sent him over the edge?

Wyatt seemed the wild card in all this. Exactly how much did he really know? And where the hell was he?

21

I'd started to doze off in the chair by the window when Billie shouted, "He's here." She bolted up, looking around with fear in her eyes. "He's in the room."

I went over and sat down on the edge of the bed. "You're dreaming," I said. "It was a nightmare. There's no one here but you and me."

She pushed her sweaty hair back from her face with both hands and kept her palms pressed down on the top of her head, wide-eyed and panting, looking like a cornered animal. A cell phone sounded in her back pocket. Its ringtone was the first few bars of the Cure song "One Hundred Years."

"Where did you find your phone?" I said.

"In my mom's handbag," she replied. "When we got to Cathy's house. She hid it from me so I wouldn't find out the truth about Janis."

"Go ahead and answer, if you want," I said. "Maybe it's Wyatt. You can find out where he is."

She reached back and removed the phone, looking at the screen. "It's not him," she said, rather unconvincingly.

"Who is it?"

"Caitlyn. The girl from the party. She's been bugging me ever since Janis was killed. I don't even really like her that much. I just went to the party because I was bored."

The phone eventually went silent. Outside, the wind sounded like banshee cries.

"What happened to Janis's phone?" I asked.

"I don't know. What do you mean?"

"I've been getting texts from it."

"That's crazy."

"They started the night you and your mom left my house. They try to point me away from you as a suspect."

"I didn't send them. The killer must have her phone."

"Why would the killer send me texts that say you're innocent?"

"How should I know? Sounds like he's playing games."

Someone knocked on the door, a loud rapping. Billie sat forward, eyes wide with fright.

"Chance, it's Caruso," the detective called in through the door. "Open up." I put a finger to my lips, motioning with my other hand for Billie to stay still. "Don't waste my time, okay," Caruso shouted. "I know you're in there. And so is the kid. Open the door."

"Don't," Billie whispered. "Please."

"I've no choice."

I stood and went to the door. I released the bolt, kept the security bar in place, and opened the door a couple of inches. Caruso stood just outside, flanked by officers Steen and Zeravsky.

"Where is she?" he said.

"Asleep," I said. "I was, too. I was going to call you in the morning. We're not going anywhere. Steen and Zeravsky can sit on the room all night if you want, to make sure."

"Yeah, giving you an entire night to prep the girl on what to say."

"I don't work that way, Dante."

He frowned. "Why should I trust anything you tell me now?"

I glanced back at Billie. She'd pushed herself back to the corner, the covers pulled around her as if this would keep her safe. "I've been asking her questions, not feeding her lines. Come back in the morning and I'll fill you in."

He made no move to leave. Behind him, spiraling dust and sand from the wind created a thick soup through which I could barely see.

"Can we talk alone?" I asked. Caruso shrugged and sighed, then motioned for the officers to return to their squad car. I closed the door, swung the security bar away, then stepped outside to join him. "She's a mess. I found her hiding in an old car in the garage of the Zeigler house. She was there when the two women were attacked. She's terrified. She just woke from a nightmare where she thought the killer was in the room with us."

"Look, Chance, I admire your determination to see the best in her. I really do. But we've got two crime scenes now, and she's the one constant. If she hid out in the house, it's because she didn't want to get caught."

"She says Adam Leary killed her sister."

Caruso frowned. "She knows this how?"

"Leary's younger son Wyatt told her."

"He's accusing his own father of murder?"

"That's what she claims."

"Why? What motive? You know, *that* pesky little thing."

"I don't know yet."

"Then you're wasting my time."

"Whoever attacked Catherine Zeigler came up from

behind," I said, "and slit her throat like this." I made a move with my hand across my own. "A left-handed cut. Shouldn't be hard to find out if Leary's a southpaw. Also, she's a tall woman, and Adam Leary is a very tall man. Billie's quite short. She'd have had to jump on Catherine's back to cut her that deeply."

"You've got an explanation for everything, don't you?" Caruso jammed his hands into the side pockets of his windbreaker and looked out across the parking lot. "Jesus, I hate the desert," he said.

I followed his gaze and looked off toward the street. A pair of headlights cruised past, the car slowing for a bit then speeding up. The dark mass of the metal moved on down the road and was swallowed up by the sand. Its appearance further unnerved me. I made a snap decision. "Okay, you win," I said. "Take her in. Arrest her right now."

"What?"

"Arrest her. Take her back to Los Angeles tonight."

"You're a Goddamned enigma, Chance. You make my head spin."

"It's for her own good," I said. "She'll be safer in your custody than here with me."

Caruso didn't argue; it's what he'd wanted all along. But Billie didn't go quietly. She fought as the officers lifted her from the bed, and she called me a bastard as they dragged her out the door.

"It's temporary," I told her. "And for your own protection. Tell me where I can find Wyatt."

"Fuck you." She spat at my feet.

Zeravsky carried her, kicking and screaming, across the parking lot. Steen helped put the young girl into the backseat. Several motel guests came out to investigate the ruckus. The elderly woman who'd checked us in stood in the window of the reception office, arms folded across her chest, shaking her head in disgust, like a schoolteacher who'd caught the janitor with his hand down a student's pants. Caruso stood in the middle of the lot and watched as the patrol SUV drove off, his hand over his nose and mouth against the sand.

"I'm going back to bed," I said to him.

"Sweet dreams," he answered, his voice muffled. "I'll be picking up the mother in the morning."

I closed and locked the door. In the bathroom, as I splashed cold water on my face, I heard the distinctive Cure song ringtone of Billie's phone. In the struggle of her arrest, she'd left the device behind; I found it tangled in the sheets of the bed. Grabbing a tissue, I used it to pick up the phone.

Wyatt Calling was displayed across the screen.

I answered without a word, hoping Wyatt would assume he'd reached Billie and start talking on his own, maybe even cue me in as to his whereabouts.

"Billie," he said. "You okay?" He paused. "Where are you? What happened? When I went to the house, there were cops all over. I guess they didn't buy it."

I couldn't afford to scare him off and have him disappear, so I said nothing and ended the call. He'd probably think we'd lost the connection. I'd have to find him another way.

I guess they didn't buy it.

The statement had ominous implications. I tried to open Billie's phone so I could look at her messages, but the device was password-protected. I slipped it into a plastic bag and stored it in my pocket, next to Janis's bird statue.

22

When I woke a few hours later, the white curtains of the motel room glowed with early morning sunlight. I stood, stretched, walked to the window, and pulled them open. The sky was clear. The sandstorm had passed. But the cars in the lot were covered with a thick coat of sand and dirt.

I went into the bathroom and washed my hands and face. Then I called Charley.

"Kathy says you're still in the desert," she said.

"Someone tried to kill Anna. They murdered her friend, Catherine Zeigler."

"Oh Lord. How did it happen?"

"I fucked up. The killer wasn't following me, he was following someone else. The texts weren't from him. I'll fill you in when I get back."

"Okay. Where's Billie?"

"Detective Caruso arrested her last night and took her back to LA. I wanted him to. She's safer behind bars."

"That makes sense. How bad is Anna?"

"I'll think she'll pull through. I'm going to stop by the hospital now, then I'm coming home."

"Good. Listen, Jagger, about the things I said ..."

"You don't owe me an explanation or any kind of apology."

"I'm up and down and all over the place. I hate it."

"Stop it. I'm the asshole for not having more patience."

"You're an asshole for a lot of reasons," she said, and chuckled. Her laugh was the sweetest sound I'd heard in a while.

"I'll see you in a few hours," I said.

"Good. I love you."

"And I love you."

Anna was awake in her hospital bed when I got there, but she looked groggy. "Where's Billie?"

"Detective Caruso came last night and arrested her."

Her jaw tensed and her eyes flared. "You promised me she'd be okay."

"And she will be. No one can get to her if she's in custody. The police can protect her better than I can. And it makes it easier for me to work."

She sank back onto the pillows. "This just gets worse and worse, doesn't it? Poor Catherine. All she did was help me. Gave me a place to stay. I never should have stopped in the desert. We should have kept going."

"The minute you crossed state lines, the feds would have gotten involved. You couldn't run forever."

"What happens now?"

"I need to find Wyatt Leary. That's step one. And I need the password to Billie's phone to do it."

"Her phone? You have it?"

"She left it in the motel room when they arrested her."

"How did *she* get it?"

"She found it in your handbag. Are you really surprised? A teen without a phone is like a junkie without a fix. What's her password? Do you know it?"

"Jabber," Anna said. "J-A-B-B-E-R. It's short for Jabberwocky. From a Lewis Carroll poem. It was her favorite as a child. She loved *Alice in Wonderland* and *Through the Looking Glass*. 'Beware the Jabberwock, my son. The jaws that bite, the claws that catch.'" The memory brought tears to Anna's eyes.

I took her hand. "I'm going to figure this out. I promise. Billie's going to be safe. I'm going to stop whoever's done this to you."

Driving back to Los Angeles, I listened to the Nine Inch Nails double album, *The Fragile*. Trent Reznor's dark lyrics and pounding industrial rock was a perfect match for my mood. I was frustrated by the case and angry at myself. I'd failed, and an innocent woman was dead because of it.

The house was empty when I got home—Kathy at school and Charley at one of her skin burn therapy sessions. I did an abbreviated meditation session, barely ten minutes, then made a grilled cheese sandwich and took it out on the back deck with a cup of coffee, pen and paper, and Billie's cell phone. As I ate, famished, I jotted down notes of everything I knew so far about the case. Notes for myself, no one else; a years-old habit that helped sort things out by putting them in order.

>*Janis murdered. Body found by sister. Billie later discovered by neighbor Marty, wandering the streets near the house, covered in blood and holding the murder weapon. LAPD arrest her.*

>Billie arraigned. Remanded into mother's custody. Billie is catatonic and remains so for nearly a week. Possibly faking. Difficult to know for sure. If so, why? Cover up? Guilt?

>I meet with LAPD detective Dante Caruso. He's not keen on a private investigation. Believes Billie's guilty. Also, he is dying of cancer. May affect his focus on case.

>Against my advice, Anna flees town with Billie after girl regains consciousness.

>I receive odd texts designed to make me think Billie's innocent and another killer is on the loose. Juvenile, melodramatic stuff. But why pull attention away from prime suspect and risk getting caught? Billie might be behind texts to throw me off.

>Teenage girl murdered in Woodland Hills. Similar MO/not exact. Texter alerts me to it. Could be killer, proving existence. Or an unconnected and random murder that the texter exploited to prove point.

>Janis's friend Isabelle claims Janis was dating Paige Leary.

>Paige denies knowing Janis. Short film he made at USC has characteristics of Janis's murder. Also, it appears father Adam Leary squelched a rape charge against Paige by giving victim an acting role on TV series. Adam Leary is facing sexual harassment charges of his own at work.

>Anna's friend Catherine Zeigler murdered in Indio. Anna attacked, as well, stabbed. Billie found hiding in car in garage. Seems genuinely terrified.

>Paige has a younger brother, Wyatt. Wyatt and Billie are close. How serious??? So far, unsuccessful in tracking Wyatt down.

>Billie claims Wyatt told her his dad killed Janis and so probably came to desert and attacked Catherine and Anna. No motive known, but possibly to kill Billie before she remembered something from that night.

>Wyatt called Billie's cell phone in the desert. He said, "I guess they didn't buy it."

I set the notes aside and picked up Billie's phone. I used the password Anna had given me—JABBER—to gain access, then I texted Wyatt from her contacts list.

Where are you? I typed, then erased and retyped, *where r u?*

back in la, he responded. *at my friends daphne & mia. u?*

coming to see u. give me address.

u don't remember?

no. just give it. i'm all messed up.

He sent me the address of an apartment on Genesee in West Hollywood.

1 hour, I texted back.

23

Wyatt had been staying with two friends, Daphne Viera and Mia Bach, since the Friday before Janis's death. They lived in a rundown mid-century apartment building on the corner of Genesee and Beverly, across from the CBS Television City center. Mia let me into the apartment holding a Rickenbacker bass guitar in her arm. Tall and thin, she had raven hair and multiple piercings on her face. Daphne—short and pudgy, with spiked blonde hair and plastic frame glasses a size too big for her small round face—sat on the floor of the living room, focused on her laptop computer screen.

Music played—"Hit Me Like a Snare" by the British art-rock band Alt-J—turned too loud for normal conversation. I had to shout to be heard as I asked about Wyatt. Daphne told me he was in the bathroom, washing up. Mia went back to practicing, playing the bass line of the song along with the recording, her bass plugged into a mini Marshall amp.

I sat down on a brick-colored armchair that looked and smelled like it had been rescued from a nearby curbside, and I tried to make conversation while I waited. Daphne, I learned, designed websites. Mia played in a punk rock band called The Zits that was just getting on its feet. Her father, I learned, was Lazarus Bach—more commonly known to fans as *Lazer*—the keyboardist for a local funk metal band called Tranceland. I knew and admired them.

"I've seen them twice," I said, "at the Roxy. And I've got their three albums on vinyl." Mia seemed pleased to hear this.

Wyatt eventually emerged from the bathroom, tensing as soon as he saw me. "Where's Billie?" he said. "What's going on?"

"Wyatt, my name is Jason Chance. I'm helping Billie and her mother, Anna."

"I know who you are. Billie told me all about you." He relaxed a little. "Is she okay?"

"She's been arrested."

"Fuck ..."

"No. It's a good thing," I said. "She's safer behind bars."

He nodded. "That kind of makes sense."

Wyatt's unkempt state seemed organic, and I couldn't help wondering what exactly "cleaning up" for him entailed. His hair was unwashed and tangled. Adolescent peach fuzz covered his chin and upper lip, with a few errant hairs creeping up his cheeks and down his neck. He wore a white T-shirt, yellowing at the collar, that was too big for his scrawny frame and made him look anorexic. His jeans were ripped and full of holes from years of wear, not a designer's whim.

"Any chance we could turn that down?" I said to Mia, who was closest to the sound system. "I love Alt-J as much as anybody, but it's kind of hard to talk." Mia shrugged and turned a knob on the player. The song quieted to a low drone. "Thank you."

"Billie must be freaking out," Wyatt said.

"It's not an ideal situation for her," I said, "but it's safer than if she was out on the street."

"I could protect her. I'm stronger than I look."

Daphne and Mia laughed at the comment.

"Fuck you both," Wyatt said.

"*Fuck you both*," Daphne imitated, making her voice high-pitched and nasally. Mia played three hard chords on her axe to accentuate.

Wyatt scowled and ran his fingers through his messy hair. "Forget them," he said to me. "They're my friends, but they're morons."

"*They're my friends, but they're morons*," Daphne mocked. Mia and she laughed in sync.

"Is there someplace we could talk in private?" I said.

"Take him to the roof," Mia said. "We don't mind."

"We won't be offended if you guys want to be alone together," Daphne added. This brought another round of giggles from the women.

I motioned for Wyatt to take the lead, then followed him out the door. We went up a flight of stairs to a pebble-and-tar roof. A low wall ran its entire perimeter, with satellite dishes lining one edge. Beyond them, I could see the sound studios of TV City spread out over several acres of prime West Hollywood real estate. Behind it, the old Farmer's Market and the upscale Grove shopping mall finished out the huge block between Beverly and Third.

Wyatt sat on the wall and took a pack of cigarettes from his socks. "Want one?" he asked, holding out the box.

"I don't smoke," I said. "You shouldn't, either."

He laughed and lit up. Blowing smoke out his mouth, he said, "So why'd you come to me? What did you want?"

I told him all that had happened in Indio.

"Is Mrs. Ryker okay?" he asked.

"I think she'll pull through. But her friend is dead."

"That sucks." He looked down at his sneakers, flicking ash from the cigarette.

"I know you were there. That you went to the house."

"Yeah, sort of. I never went in. And I never saw Billie. By the time I got to the house, whatever happened had already gone down. Cops were all over the place." He took a drag. "You don't think I had anything to do with any of it, do you? I didn't hurt anybody, I swear to God. I waited in my car a couple of blocks away. Billie was supposed to come to me, but she never did."

Whoever followed Wyatt to Indio must have cruised the neighborhood after Wyatt parked, looking for Anna's car. A vintage red Volvo wouldn't be too hard to spot.

"After an hour, I walked over," Wyatt said. "When I saw the cops, I figured it meant she and her mom got caught."

"What did you do then?"

"What could I do? Nothing. I went back to my car, then I came back here." His confusion seemed sincere, as did his fear, but that could have been motivated by many things.

"Billie's told me a lot," I said. "But not everything, I suspect. Maybe you can fill in the blanks."

He shrugged and smoked.

"Why do you think your father killed Janis?" I asked.

The question caught him off guard. "Billie said that?"

"It's okay. You can trust me. I'm on your side. And Billie's."

He looked off toward an electronic billboard on Beverly that changed images every thirty seconds, advertising different CBS television shows. East-to-west traffic on the large street below was backed up. The blaring of horns filled the air, sounding like an out-of-tune brass section in an orchestra.

"I heard him talking on the phone," he said, at last. "He was saying how he'd offered someone money for silence about something but they wouldn't go along with it. So he was going to have to up his game."

"Who was he speaking with?"

"I don't know. Paige maybe. Or Angelique, his personal assistant. He vents everything to her because he has her by the throat. He knows she'll never turn on him."

"Why not?"

"She owes him. She's from Haiti. You know, one of the beautiful places Dictator Trump called 'shitholes.' Dad arranged for her to have her papers to stay here in the US. I think they're fake. He probably threatens her with deportation if she doesn't do everything he says."

"Your father paid someone off six months ago. A sixteen-year-old girl. Gave her a role on his TV show. I think it was to protect Paige. Maybe he was referring to that in the phone call?"

"No, this was something different. He was talking in the present tense."

"When did this conversation happen?"

"A couple of days before Janis was killed. He thought he was alone in the house. Paige was out, and I was supposed to go to Laguna with Mia and The Zits for a gig. I do sound work for them. But I overslept and missed the ride."

"So by upping his game, you think he meant murder?"

"Yeah. What else?"

"Could mean a lot of things."

"He sounded ... dangerous when he said it."

"Still, killing somebody is a pretty extreme action. You believe your father is capable of that?"

"To protect himself or someone else important, sure."

"Paige, maybe?" I paused. "Did your brother rape Janis?"

"I wouldn't put it past him."

"So your father killed Janis to cover that up?" It seemed farfetched.

"My dad adores Paige. As far as he's concerned, that asshole can do no wrong."

"And what about you?"

"Dad never wanted me. I was an accident. I think I was the reason he and mom eventually got divorced." He tried to sound nonchalant and almost pulled it off. I sensed rage seething underneath.

"When you called Billie last night and said, *I guess they didn't buy it*, what did you mean?"

"That was you who answered?" he said. "I wondered. Billie would've said something, even if she couldn't really talk. Given me a clue or something. To let me know she was okay." He tossed the cigarette off the side of the roof and leaned over to watch it fall to the street below. He made the sound of an explosion as the butt hit the asphalt.

"Answer my question."

"*I guess they didn't buy* that there was another killer out there," he said. "I thought she'd been arrested when I said it."

"You sent me the texts? From Janis's phone, to make me believe Billie is innocent?"

"She *is* innocent," he said, standing up. "Yeah, it was me. I wanted to create reasonable doubt. The moron police seem so sure it's her. When I read about that other murder, the one in Woodland Hills, it seemed too good not to use. I mean, it was terrible what happened to that girl and all. I just wanted to help Billie."

"You could have told the police about your father."

"I've got no proof. Who's going to believe me? They'd just think I was trying to protect my girlfriend. It would be a waste of time. My dad's smarter than all of you." He choked up saliva and spat, then started a slow walk along the wall, kicking debris out of his way as he moved. It felt like he suddenly wanted to get away from me. And my questions.

"Is that the only reason?" I asked.

"What do you mean?" He kept walking, his back to me.

"Billie backed you into a corner when she revealed to me what you thought about your dad," I said, following him. "So you *had* to tell me today. And you only confessed it to her so she'd go along with your plan."

He turned and glared at me. "What plan?" Looking in his eyes, I knew I was right. Another piece clicked into place.

"It won't work, kid," I said. "You're too young and foolish to pull it off."

"What are you talking about?"

"You don't want to turn your father in, you want to blackmail him, so he'll give you something in return for your silence. I'm guessing money. Maybe so you and Billie can run away."

"That's bullshit," he said, not very convincingly.

"But you can't outrun the guilt, Wyatt, no matter how far you go."

"I've got nothing to feel guilty about." But he did, and he knew it, even if he wouldn't admit it. He'd inadvertently led a killer to the desert. Because of that, a woman was dead.

"You want to help Billie, tell the police what you know about your father," I said. "Come with me to see Detective Caruso. Tell him everything you overheard. Let the LAPD find the proof to back it up."

Wyatt took out another cigarette and lit it. This time, his hands trembled, and the flame of his lighter shook. "I didn't hear anything," he finally said, and blew smoke in my face. "I made it all up. Just now. For Billie's sake. To protect her. I never heard my dad say anything. It was all a lie." He turned and stalked across the roof to the exit door, pushed through it, and was gone.

24

Caruso and I sat side-by-side at a metal table in the center of an interrogation room of the Van Nuys Police Station. A female officer led Billie in. She'd been brought down from the Barry J. Nidorf Juvenile Hall in Sylmar where they were holding her. The officer shut the door, unlocked Billie's handcuffs, then took up a position in a corner, standing and staring at the wall. Billie dropped onto the chair across from us. She looked like she'd aged five years after a night of incarceration.

"How's my mom?" she asked.

"I called over to the hospital earlier," I said. "She's stronger today and has even been able to eat a little."

"When will they let her come home?"

"They don't know yet. The knife wound was deep and did a fair amount of internal damage. Those kinds of injuries take time to heal."

"Did you arrest Wyatt's dad?"

"No, Billie, we haven't," Caruso said. "The police are going to need more than Wyatt's say-so. And he hasn't even said so to anybody but you."

"Why would he make something like that up about his own father?" Billie said.

"Maybe because he's in love with you," Caruso said, "and hopes he can protect you."

"He does love me. And I love him. But he wouldn't lie."

"Why do you trust him so much?" I asked.

She thought a bit before answering, her eyes roaming from Caruso to me and finally to her hands on the tabletop. "He's the only one who's ever understood me," she said, at last. "Why I'm the way I am."

"What way is that?" Caruso said.

She looked back at him, a change coming over her, as if all her anger, fear, and sadness in that moment channeled down to a single emotion: hatred. If she'd had a gun to point at Caruso's head, I suspect she would have pulled the trigger. "You wouldn't get it. The contradictions would baffle you."

"I bet they would, at that," Caruso said.

"Try me," I said, leaning forward.

She tapped two fingers on the tabletop, a staccato rhythm, barely audible, as she held my gaze. "Everything about me is in a song, 'One Hundred Years.' It's by The Cure. Listen to that, you'll understand."

The song on her ringtone. The song Kathy heard in her dream.

"I doubt that's true," I said. "No one's life is ever summed up by one thing. Not even by a beautiful and profound song. But I know the one you mean. And I think I know why you'd say it was about you. You're the black-haired girl Robert Smith sings about, right? What's the *death blow* you're waiting for? What is it that feels like *one hundred years*?" I paused. "Is it the loss of your father?"

Billie bit her bottom lip, fighting valiantly against tears. "I miss him every day." She wiped her sleeve across her nose and mouth. "Are your mom and dad still alive?"

"No. My mother died when I was young. My father, a few years ago."

"It probably hurts less as you get older."

"Don't bet on it." I held her stare. She couldn't last and broke our eye contact, turning her head and looking at the wall.

"I can't stay another night in jail," she said. "It's like sleeping in hell."

"You're safer than if you were out," I said.

"According to you." She dropped her head down on her arms on the table. "I'm not lying about anything." Her words were muted by the cloth of her shirt. "Neither is Wyatt."

"We need more than that," Caruso said.

"What do you want me to do? Wyatt's the one who knows things, not me."

"He admits he's got no proof to back his claim," I said. "And I think he has another agenda. To blackmail his father into giving you both money to run away."

Billie chortled. "Like that would ever happen. And even if he thought about it, so what? He pointed you in the right direction. Isn't it up to you guys to find the proof?" She wasn't being defiant; she sounded desperate.

"Did you ever meet Paige or his father?" I asked.

"No."

"Did Janis ever meet his dad?"

"I don't know!" She buried her head back in her elbow.

I glanced over at Caruso, who was shaking his head. "This is a waste of my time," he said, and turned to the officer in the corner. "Take her back to Juvie."

Billie suddenly sat up, her eyes opening wide. "Wait!"

"What is it?" I asked. "What's wrong?"

"I remember something! About that night. About coming home."

"You've got to be kidding me," Caruso said.

"I swear. It just came to me. Because of all we're talking about. Just popped into my head. Right now. Like a ... flash. Isn't that the way memory works?"

"It's the way a lot of things work," Caruso said. "Lies, too."

She pushed back against the table. "You don't want to hear it, fine. Take me back. Go ahead."

I said, "Tell me what you remember."

"Why bother? Mister Know It All here won't believe it. He doesn't believe anything except his own mind. Which he's already made up."

"I promise it will stay as open as possible," Caruso said, tapping his forehead.

"And I really want to hear," I said.

Billie sat forward. "I remember walking home from the party," she said. "I had to walk uphill to get there. It was so hot. A car approached, coming down. It slowed as it got close to me. At first, I could see only the high beam headlights shining in my eyes. They were kind of blinding. As the car passed, I saw what kind it was. A blue Prius. It was Wyatt's car."

"How do you know?" I asked.

"He's got a COEXIST bumper sticker on the front. And a skeleton hanging from the rearview mirror. But Wyatt wasn't driving."

"Who was behind the wheel?" I asked.

"I couldn't see a face through the tinted windows.

Someone taller than Wyatt, for sure. His head almost touched the ceiling."

"You could see that and the skeleton but not the driver's face?" Caruso said.

"The skeleton's day-glo red. It stands out. And the driver was just a tall silhouette. No way it was Wyatt. He had a gig that night with his friend's band. The Zits. At the Troubadour. He went with them in the van. I remember that, too."

"Yeah, you're suddenly a wealth of information," Caruso said.

Billie looked at me. "I told you he wouldn't believe it."

"Excuse me for being skeptical," Caruso said. "But all of a sudden you remember stuff that miraculously backs up your claim? I'm a fool but not an idiot."

"It's like you *want* me to be guilty."

"No, kid, I don't. But look where we are."

"Everything's been a blank until this minute," Billie said. "That's not my fault. And I can't control what suddenly comes back into my head."

"Anything else out of the ordinary about the car?" I asked.

Billie shook her head. "The driver's window was closed. And the glass was smoked. I couldn't see inside. But it must have been Wyatt's dad. He took that car so nobody would connect things back to him. Who else? It makes perfect sense."

"Nothing about this makes sense," Caruso said. "And I'm done for now." He motioned again for the guard to take Billie away. The young girl went silent as she was led out, with barely a glance back at me as the door swung shut.

. . .

OUT IN THE CENTER OF THE COURTHOUSE COMPLEX, CARUSO and I bought cups of coffee from an ambulatory vendor, then walked to Delano Street, where we'd left our cars in the main courthouse parking structure.

"She really knows how to spin it," Caruso said.

"If she was going to make something up, why tell us she saw Wyatt's car?"

"So we'd buy it. Would've been too obvious and suspicious to just say, *I saw Adam Leary*. She's clever for her age. They all are these days. Too clever. The world's changing. Thank you, social media and absentee parenting."

"Anna is anything but an absentee parent," I said.

"Yet one girl was a slut and the other a killer."

I felt my shoulders go rigid. My right hand balled into a fist. "Say something like that again and I won't think twice about knocking the shit out of you."

"Jesus, Chance, calm down." He sighed. "Sorry. You're right. It was out of line. I'm just tired of this whole damned thing."

"You really won't give her an inch, will you? Are you that afraid of being wrong?"

"I resent that, Chance. I said it to you from the beginning. Bring me proof. Not innuendo. No made-up stories. Proof."

He crossed the street and headed up the staircase to the second floor of the parking lot, struggling as he climbed the steps, his shoulders rising and falling as his cancer-riddled lungs labored to breathe. I felt for the man. He wanted this case to end so he could die in peace. At the same time, he wanted to die knowing for sure he got his last one right. And while he fought for a meaningful death, Billie fought for her life. I believed her story about the night of the murder. And it gave me an idea.

. . .

ADAM LEARY ANSWERED THE DOOR OF HIS SOUTHERN-STYLE mansion this time, and he didn't look happy to see me.

"Anna Ryker and her friend were attacked yesterday in a home near Palm Springs," I said. "Anna's in the hospital, and the other woman is dead."

"That's terrible news. What does it have to do with me or my family?"

"May I come in? There's something I think you need to know."

Adam took a business card from his wallet and held it out to me. "This is the name and number of my attorney. If you've got questions about anything concerning my family, take it up with him." He slammed shut the door.

I stepped back, looking over at a large window of frosted glass, one of two that flanked the front door. Leary's silhouette passed across it. Pressing my ear to the glass, I heard muted voices inside—two of them, both male. I took out my cell, searched for a number, and called it. The ringtone from inside the house was loud and shrill even through the wall, a replication of the sound old rotary phones made many years ago. Paige answered after three of them.

"What's up, Mr. Chance?" he said, sounding as nonchalant as someone getting a call from a work colleague.

"Tell your father not to be foolish. He shouldn't put lawyers between us right now. I have reason to believe someone's trying to frame him. And you may end up collateral damage." I was playing a dicey game, but people who feel cornered tend to make mistakes, and cases are often solved when they do. Unfortunately, people often die, as well.

A few seconds passed, then Paige opened the front door.

"I like your style, Mr. Chance," he said. "Tough, determined. Only mildly cynical. I read up on you. Your story would make a hell of a movie. Sell me the rights, I'll make you famous."

"That's a conversation for another day. Right now, I need to talk to your father about Anna and Janis Ryker."

We sat in the backyard, on comfortable patio furniture under a white pagoda with hanging baskets of bougainvillea plants and a ceiling fan that turned slowly and silently above us. Paige was cool and sanguine, Adam tense and on guard.

"Billie claims she's started to remember details of the night her sister died," I said to Adam. "She says she saw you leave the Ryker house."

"Well, that's ridiculous," Adam said. "She's lying."

"Maybe. She claims you were driving your son Wyatt's car. A blue Prius."

"I don't drive my son's cars. I have a much nicer one of my own."

"I'm sure you do, Mr. Leary. Anybody you can think of who'd want to see you take a fall?"

"Show me a successful man in this town who doesn't have enemies, and I'll show you a liar," Adam said. "This is a witch hunt. And you're not a cop. You're only playing at being a private eye. I think this whole conversation is designed to see if I break. I've written the scene many times."

"Billie claims she actually saw my father leave her house in my brother's car?" Paige said. "After Janis was killed?"

I nodded, keeping my eyes on Adam.

"In this absurd scenario, I killed her sister? Is that what she's implying?" Adam said. "Why? What's my motive?"

"Billie thinks Paige raped Janis," I said. "And you're cleaning up for him."

"That's the craziest thing I've ever heard." Adam said.

"It sure as hell is," Paige said.

"Janis told her a couple of days before she was killed that you tried to buy her silence." *If you're going to roll the dice, roll 'em big. A lie is only a lie to someone who knows the truth.*

Adam's face turned the color of the flowers hanging above him. "This is outrageous."

"I'm just telling you what Billie claimed her sister said. It could all be invented, but if she's trying to beat a murder rap, she needs to create a plausible motive for another killer, right?"

"Key word being *plausible*," Paige said. "I didn't rape anybody. I don't need to force women to make love to me."

"Shut up, Paige." Adam said. "Has Billie told these suspicions to the police?"

"I can't answer that," I said.

"Can't or won't?"

"Detective Caruso is keeping me at arms' length about everything. He doesn't like that I'm investigating. He thinks I'm stepping all over his case. But Billie seems to trust me more than she trusts him."

"Caruso doesn't know you're here?" Paige said.

"I just wanted to warn you, give you a heads-up."

"Why would you care?" Adam asked.

"I'm interested in nailing the real killer. I don't ever like seeing someone take the heat for something they didn't do." I stood. "I appreciate your taking the time to listen. I'll see myself out."

Driving away, I felt a little dirty, like a criminal who'd just set in motion his most lurid crime. Oddly enough, I was also exhilarated, working without the constraints of the police code. Hopefully, I'd rattled Leary enough for him to make a stupid move. I needed more than I had so far if I wanted to get Billie freed. And at least she was safe from any possible repercussions.

Kathy phoned as I reached Melrose and Crescent Heights. "I had another dream," she said. "About Janis."

I could no longer discount the fact that my daughter's dreams had eerily mirrored aspects of the case, so I was eager for her to describe this new one.

"We were in her house," Kathy said, "and it was night. Janis and I were alone in her bedroom, and we were playing music. The Janis Joplin album. The one hanging over her bed."

"*Pearl*," I said.

"Yeah. The song didn't have any vocals, though, just the band playing. A sort of up-tempo blues thing."

"'Buried Alive in the Blues.'"

"What?"

"The name of the song. 'Buried Alive in the Blues.' It's the only instrumental piece on the album."

"Is there anything you *don't* know about rock music?"

"Plenty, believe me."

"Weird that I would dream about something I didn't know or have never heard, isn't it?"

"Yes. Tell me more."

"Janis was sitting on her bed, holding the album cover. She was in her underwear, a white bra and panties that were covered in blood. You could see the puncture wounds from the attack all over her chest and abdomen. It was gross. But in the dream, it didn't seem to bother me. At one point, I lay back on the floor, clapping along with the music. Suddenly, blood started to splatter across the ceiling above me, like someone had flicked it. A few drops even landed on my cheeks. I sat up and looked at Janis. She was ripping the album cover apart, and blood was flying out of it in all directions. All over her, across the walls, up on the ceiling. It was as if the whole thing had turned to blood. I woke up crying. I still can't shake the feeling it gave me."

"I'm sorry you're going through this," I said, "even if they are only dreams."

"Dad, it's a good thing. I'm positive Janis is telling us something."

"You know what, Katbird? I'm starting to agree."

We ended the call, and I headed west. Pacific Coast Highway from Santa Monica would take me to Malibu Canyon, which became Topanga Canyon Road halfway through. It would be a quicker drive to Anna's house than going through the valley. And the route would help clear my head. Even in traffic, there's something rejuvenating about driving along the edge of the Pacific Ocean.

The mid-afternoon sun peeked out from wispy clouds over the blue green sea to my left. I rolled down the windows and breathed in salt air. An old song by TV on the Radio played on the satellite station, "Family Tree." At the intersection of Sunset Boulevard and Pacific Coast Highway, a guy on a Harley had collided with a pickup truck. The accident forced two lanes into one, the merging made slower by each driver's determination to get a good, long look at the scene as he or she passed. The biker lay on his back, immobilized, in a head brace, while paramedics tended to him. His bike was nearby, on its side across the center line. The front tire had popped free from its struts, and the frame was twisted like an abstract metal sculpture. It reminded me of Lenny's artwork on Anna's front lawn, and I thought how an image can be beautiful in one light, horrifying and tragic in another.

The damaged truck was parked in the lot of Patrick's Roadhouse, its left side crushed in from what must have been a high-speed impact. The driver, an elderly man wearing a Dodgers jersey and a sweat-stained orange cap pushed up high on his forehead, leaned against the door, looking shaken. For a second, our eyes met as I drove past. The old man lifted up his free hand and gave me the finger. I turned my gaze front and drove on.

A sudden distraction or a slick patch of road, and the lives of two men are altered, perhaps irreparably. In the time it takes to breathe, everything can change. Our guardian angels look away, and tragedy hits. We live at the mercy of chance.

I TURNED ONTO HORSESHOE LANE AND DROVE TO THE TOP OF the hill. The police car was no longer parked in front of Anna's house, meaning I no longer had to sneak around. I climbed the front yard steps, jumped the side gate, and went around to the back. At the kitchen door, I reached in past the shards of broken glass from my last break-in, unlocked the door, and entered.

In Janis's room, I took the framed *Pearl* album cover off the wall, turned it over, flipped up the small metal brackets that held the protective backing in place, and removed the album cover. The cardboard sleeve was flimsy, with no LP inside. I buckled it open and shined my phone's flashlight in the slit. Four small sheets of paper were lodged inside.

Using a tissue from a bedside box, I carefully removed the pages. My stomach tightened as I looked down at photographic images, sexual in nature, of Janis and Adam Leary together in bed.

25

The location shown in the photos was not Janis's bedroom, but another one in some other house. The pictures—on plain paper printed from a computer—were crumpled and torn at the edges. A single word had been handwritten across each, in red marker.

Slut. Pig. Bitch. Corpse.

I went to the kitchen and retrieved two plastic bags from the cupboard above the stove: one sandwich-size, the other gallon-size. I put the photos into the smaller bag. The album cover wouldn't fit in the larger one, so I had to use a trash bag I found under the sink. I took this new evidence out to my car, locked it in the trunk, then called Caruso.

"What's wrong now?" he said.

"There's something you need to see."

I MET WITH HIM AT A COFFEE SHOP A FEW BLOCKS FROM THE Van Nuys Courthouse and Municipal Building. While I drank strong coffee and he ate a tuna salad sandwich, I told him about my conversations with the Learys.

"Damn, Chance," Caruso said. "You've sure gone rogue. How'd the old man react?"

"Denial. Threatened me with lawyers."

"They always do."

"But I think he's rattled."

"About a lot of things," Caruso said. "Leary just got fired from his Netflix show because of the sexual harassment thing. On top of that, two female production assistants have come forward claiming he forced them to give him oral sex in the office, threatening to fire them and ruin their careers if they refused."

"God bless the Me Too movement," I said. "No more fear."

"There's still fear, but it's getting better." He fought off a coughing attack and drank some water. "What about the son, Paige? How did he react to your brace?"

"Cool as Malibu in winter."

Caruso chuckled then shook his head. "Don't know why I'm laughing."

"It gets worse," I said.

I showed him the photos I'd retrieved from Janis's bedroom. He studied the pictures a long time before responding, looking at each one carefully before moving on to the next—not in any seedy or voyeuristic way, but as a methodical cop studying new evidence. Finally, he tossed them on the table, sat back, crossed his arms, and frowned.

"Well, that just killed my appetite," he said.

"Is this enough for you?" I asked. "Are you ready to consider I've been right? That Billie is innocent?"

"Yeah, Jason, I am. And I'm gonna look like an asshole when we come out on the other side."

"If things turn out as they should, I will gladly stay in the shadows. You take the collar, you take the credit. That's not what this is about for me."

"Right. I forgot. You're a modern-day Robin Hood." He paused. "By the way, that Woodland Hills murder?"

"Natalie Cara?"

"Yeah. They got the guy. The victim's ex-boyfriend. He copped to the murder last night. Did it because she'd dumped him. So whoever sent those texts to you must have read about the murder and used it to try and influence your suspicions." He studied my reaction. Or lack of one. "You don't seem surprised."

"Wyatt Leary admitted he sent the texts. He thought he was helping Billie."

Caruso sadly shook his head. "Amazing how these kids can be so smart and so stupid at the same time."

"There's no age limit on foolishness."

"Yeah, I guess not."

"You really don't like kids, do you?" I said.

"No, Jason, I don't. Maybe just because they're young and I'm old and dying." He pushed his plate away. "Looks like Adam Leary was covering up his own crime, not his son's."

"So you're ready to believe he killed Janis."

"I'm certainly leaning in that direction, now."

"What are you going to do?"

Caruso gathered up the photos and put them back in the plastic bag. "Have a talk with him."

And if he'd gotten to the Leary home an hour earlier than he did, he might have had a chance to do that.

ADAM LEARY'S PERSONAL ASSISTANT, ANGELIQUE TOURNEAU —the Haitian woman I'd spoken with the first time I went to the home—found the body in his study. He'd been shot in the face. She told the police the front door was locked when she arrived from running errands, and all the windows and the back door were closed.

"His face was completely obliterated," Caruso told me in a phone call to bring me up to speed. "A handgun lay on the floor by the desk chair, where it fell from his hand. There's no note or anything."

I felt a queasiness in my belly. Suicide always troubles me. A few years back, my father, a vice cop, shot himself in the head. I'd recently learned some shady things about him that helped me understand why he'd done it, but that didn't make the memory any less painful. Now I had to live with the fact that I'd perhaps pushed Adam Leary to take the same way out.

Or someone else wanted to make it look like he had.

"Paige is missing," Caruso said. "Please tell me you know where Wyatt is."

26

Caruso had already arrived outside Mia and Daphne's apartment when I pulled up. He sat on a fire hydrant, waiting.

"Things sure didn't play out the way I expected," he said.

"Do they ever?" I said.

"And now one of the scumbags is dead."

"At least we know Billie didn't kill him."

The second-floor corridor of the building smelled of fried fish, sautéing onions, and weed. Down the hall, a baby cried, and a desperate mother shouted for it to be quiet.

"You're back," Daphne said to me, opening the apartment door, looking like she'd just woken up.

"We need to speak with Wyatt," I told her.

"He's asleep. Come on in."

Smoke and the thick, musky odor of marijuana floated in the air. Mia had passed out on the sofa, hugging her bass to her chest like a lover. Wyatt was curled up in a beanbag chair by the balcony door. I leaned over him and shook his shoulder, calling his name. It took a bit to rouse the boy.

When he finally opened his red eyes and stared up at me, he said, "Who are you?"

"Jason Chance, remember? We need you to get up."

He pushed himself to a sitting position. "What's going on?"

"Where's your brother?" I asked.

"I don't know. Why?"

Mia stirred and woke. Her movement caused the bass—still plugged in—to rumble.

"Your father's dead, kid," Caruso said in a deadpan voice. "I'm Detective Dante Caruso, Los Angeles Police Department."

Wyatt stared at him, then back at me. He seemed more confused than shocked. He rubbed his bleary eyes.

"I'm sorry," I said.

"How did it happen?"

"Either he shot himself or somebody else did," Caruso said.

"Man, that's cold," Daphne said. "Sorry, dude."

"We'll need you to come with us to identify the body," Caruso said.

"Do I have to?" Wyatt said.

"You're the only relative around," Caruso said. "Unless you can tell us where Paige is."

"No idea," Wyatt said.

"Then come on," Caruso said. "Let's go." He stepped back to give Wyatt room to stand. The boy had trouble rising out of the low, flimsy chair. I took hold of his arm and helped him to his feet.

"Sorry about your dad," Mia said. "That's messed up." She set the bass aside, her thumbs strumming several strings as she did. The sound was discordant and eerie.

"My father was a bastard," Wyatt said. "I'm glad he's gone."

THE MEDICAL EXAMINER'S OFFICE ON MISSION ROAD IN Lincoln Heights was built of orange brick and tan stone, and it rose up to a rounded peak. Its vaguely gothic style looked out of place next to the modern parking structure beside it and the Chevron gas station across the street, yet it seemed fitting for a workplace where one of the daily functions was the dissection of the dead. Inside, Caruso, Wyatt, and I were sent to a waiting room.

"How come your partner never comes along?" I asked Caruso.

"He thinks you and your investigation are a waste of time. I'm sparing you having to hear him say it to your face."

"Oh," I said. "Then thanks."

A middle-aged man who looked like he hadn't seen daylight or eaten a decent meal in some time joined us. He carried a white binder filled with plastic sheets that held photographs. Classical music played from small speakers mounted in each corner of the room, the music intentionally soothing.

Most people think the identification of a loved one or family member is done by pulling a table out of a freezer or lifting a sheet off the deceased as it lies on a steel table, but that's the stuff of cop shows and action movies. More times than not, the process is done in a room like this, via photograph, far removed from the corpse. The showing of an actual body is a gruesome undertaking, so it's only done in necessary cases or when the family member specifically requests a viewing.

Caruso told the man, whose name was Skinner, that

Wyatt would be doing the identifying. Skinner asked Wyatt if he'd like some water. Wyatt shook his head. He declined an offer to sit down, as well. "I just want to get this over with."

Skinner then warned him that that the photographs were disturbing. "It also may be difficult to make a positive ID."

"Why?" Wyatt asked.

"The victim took a nearly point-blank shot to the head," Caruso said. "There isn't much left of his face."

Wyatt turned to me. "Do I have to do this?"

"Closest living relative, that's the law," Caruso said.

"There is another way," I said, and turned to Skinner. "You take pictures of the whole body, right?"

"That's correct," Skinner said.

"In cases like this, he can identify his father by physical signs," I said.

"Is that true?" Wyatt said. "I mean, I may hate the man, but I don't really want to look at a face that's been obliterated by a gunshot. Not even his."

Caruso shrugged. "Okay by me."

"Does he have any specific markings anywhere?" I asked Wyatt.

"On his left forearm," Wyatt said. "There's a tattoo of a peace sign."

Skinner opened the binder and turned over several plastic sheets attached to three large rings until he found what he was looking for. He slipped the photo out of the sheath and handed it to Caruso. The detective never glanced at the picture as he passed it to Wyatt. I looked over the boy's shoulder at the image.

There was no peace sign tattoo on the arm of this photographed body.

"You sure these are the right ones?" I said. "You didn't maybe mix them up?"

"All the info's on the back," Skinner said, sounding indignant. He was a man who took pride in his work. Every ME I'd ever worked with did.

"That's not him," Wyatt said, at last.

"The fuck you say," Caruso muttered, stepping closer to look.

"It should be here," Wyatt said, tapping a finger on the photo. "The tattoo. That's not my dad."

"Son of a bitch," Caruso said.

"Looks like Adam Leary bought himself some escape time," I said.

27

Caruso drove us back to West Hollywood, where I'd left my car. On the way, he put a rush order on fingerprint identification of the body found at the Hancock Park house. Having never met or laid eyes on Adam Leary, the detective had no way of knowing the victim at the crime scene *wasn't* Paige and Wyatt's father. Leary's personal assistant, Angelique Tourneau, the woman who claimed to have found the body and who said it was Adam Leary, was most likely in on the deception.

Caruso requested arrest warrants for both Adam and Angelique.

"Where might your father go, kid?" he asked Wyatt.

"No idea," Wyatt said, staring out the window of Caruso's sedan. His body vibrated like a live wire of electricity. I could practically smell fear coming out of his pours, drenching him in nervous sweat. Maybe he was just freaked out by the turn of events. As the sedan pulled to the curb on Genesee, he jumped out and hurried to the sidewalk, distancing himself from us.

I called after him, "Don't go up yet, Wyatt. I need to talk

to you." He grimaced and rolled his eyes, but stayed at the corner of the building, reaching down to grab the pack of cigarettes from his sock.

Caruso looked at a text that had come in. "The wound to the face of the victim in Leary's study came from the pellets of a 12-gauge shotgun shell. The handgun on the floor was left as a prop."

"Find that shotgun, you've got evidence against Adam. He killed a man to stage his own death."

"Leary's on a plane to Brazil by now, my guess. Or some other country where there's no extradition. With the Tourneau woman. Maybe Paige, too."

"He's got to realize we'll figure out the truth pretty quickly."

"Which is why he's probably moving fast. Like you said, he just needed to buy some escape time."

I got out of his sedan then looked back in through the open passenger window. "What about Billie?"

"Guess I'm cutting her loose."

"I don't want to put a target on her back. I'm the one who told Leary she'd identified him."

"Jason, he's long gone."

"Please, just do me a favor. Keep her another twenty-four hours."

"Once I present this evidence to the DA's office, they'll want to kick her loose."

"So sit on it for a day."

"No way, compadre. No can do."

"Then let me pick her up. Don't release her before I can get there."

"Two hours," he said. "Best I can do." His car screeched away from the curb, made a right turn on Beverly, and disappeared.

I joined Wyatt and told him Billie was going to be released.

"So, it's over," he said. "She's off the hook."

"It would seem that way."

"What's wrong then? You still look worried."

"I want to know where your brother is, that's all. I don't like loose ends."

"He's probably screwing one of his girlfriends and doesn't even know about Dad."

"There's something else," I said. I told him about the sex photos I'd found hidden in Janis's room.

"That's just sick," he said. "My dad is a pervert. You know about all the shit people are saying, right? The sexual harassment charges and everything."

"I've read the stories," I said. "Whoever sent the photos to Janis wrote nasty notes, as well. Calling her slut, bitch, pig. And corpse."

"Who would do that?"

"I was hoping you'd know."

"Me? How?"

"Who took them, Wyatt? It wasn't your father. The pictures were taken from a clandestine place. Like something someone would do when they planned to blackmail someone else."

Wyatt stared at me, frozen in place, trying hard not to show any emotion. He couldn't sustain the cover. His wall finally broke.

"I can't do this anymore," he muttered, and leaned back against the building.

I led him down the block to my car and helped him into the passenger seat.

"Where are we going?" he asked.

"My place," I said, as we pulled away from the curb.

He nodded, a low moan vibrating in his throat.

"Tell me about the night Janis was killed. Where were you?"

"The Zits had a show at the Troubadour. I was running sound. Billie called me from the party and told me she felt weird, and it scared her. She couldn't explain, but the feeling was unlike anything she'd ever experienced. Later, when I learned what happened that night, I wondered if maybe she'd had a premonition of Janis's death."

"When did she call you?"

"It was right after the band's set, so it must have been around eleven or so."

"Did you talk to her after she'd gone home? After the body had been found?"

"No. I tried to, but her phone was shut off. The next morning, when I heard what had happened to Janis, I was worried sick. I couldn't get in touch with Billie. And I couldn't just go over. Her mom didn't even know we were friends. Billie always said she wouldn't have liked it. I was nervous to reach out. Then I learned she'd been arrested."

"She says she saw your car on the road, driving away from her house, while she walked home the night Janis was killed. The memory just came back to her."

"It wasn't me driving. No way. I was at the Troubadour from 9 o'clock until about two in the morning. The whole band will back me up. I went in their van. They picked me up and dropped me off."

"So you're saying your father drove your car when he went to kill Janis."

"Must be. I'd left it at the house. Why take your own car to a murder, right?"

"Problem is, that's not proof. It's supposition."

He turned and looked out the window. "I don't know what else to tell you."

"How did Janis and your father end up in bed together?" When he hesitated, I said, "I need to know everything."

"One night when she showed up unannounced, Paige and she got into a big fight, and he told her to stop calling him and coming over. Janis didn't take it well. Dad was there, and I guess he played the comforting adult. I took off before anything happened, so I didn't see, but I can imagine. He'd let her tell him how she felt. He'd give her a drink and the booze would be laced. It's what he did. It's what he would always do."

"You never thought to turn him in?"

"Why bother? He'd just wiggle out of it. He has good lawyers. Then he'd probably throw me out. Or worse. I was scared I'd end up getting fucked over."

"So you came up with the plan to blackmail him."

He paused. "Billie had this dream of living in London. She says all the great music comes from there. And she hates LA. I was down with it, because I hate my dad and wanted to get away from him. Plus, this city can be a drag. Since I knew he forced girls who worked for him to have sex or they'd get fired, and that sometimes he drugged them, I came up with the idea to take pictures then blackmail him with them. After we'd left town, I planned to send the proof to the cops. I'd rob him *then* turn him in. Best of both worlds. I rigged a camera in his bedroom. Of course, I didn't know at the time that Janis would end up being the girl."

"Did Billie know?"

"No, no, no. After I saw it was Janis in the photos, I hid them and never said anything. Not until the other night, when she called from Indio. I told her then. I felt I had to."

"So you lied before about thinking your father was

covering up for Paige. You knew that wasn't the case. He was covering up his own crime."

"I didn't want you to figure out what I'd been planning to do."

"Why'd you send the photos to Janis?"

"I didn't. When I went to look for them after I heard Janis was dead, they were gone. I don't know who found them and took them. I swear that. My dad, maybe."

"Why would he send them to Janis? Why would he write those words?"

"No idea. It doesn't make sense."

He was right; it didn't. And I had another suspicion.

28

Billie looked surprised to see me waiting for her when she came through the metal doors of the juvenile detention center.

"Are you taking me to my mom?" she asked.

"Not tonight," I said. "You can stay at my house. Perhaps we can go in the morning."

She didn't argue, most likely too exhausted and overwhelmed by a couple of nights in prison to have much fight left in her. We walked toward the parking lot. A warm breeze blew leaves and plastic wrappers across our path.

"Jail sucks," she said, kicking at a bent soda can, sending it clattering across the asphalt.

"Yes Billie, sure does. But now you're out." I told her Wyatt was okay and that she would finally get to see him. She was relieved to hear it. As we drove to Valley Village, I asked, "Did you talk to Janis that night? Before what happened?"

Billie shook her head. "I wish I had, now. She was in her room when I left for the party, talking on the phone to somebody with her door closed. She sounded angry. I could hear her shouting. Even if I'd tried to say goodbye, she wouldn't have paid attention to me." She paused. "I'm glad I don't remember finding her. I don't know how I could deal with that."

"We learn to deal with a lot of things we don't think we'll be able to," I said.

"I guess. I hope."

"Who was Janis fighting with? Do you know? Was it Paige?"

Billie shrugged. "They'd broken up way before that night."

"Why?"

"I don't know. I think because she was too needy and Paige got fed up. That's what Wyatt said. She didn't talk to me about him. She didn't tell me much of anything." I heard sadness in this last comment, and my heart ached for her. "I know about the photos Wyatt took. Of Janis with his dad."

"Wyatt's blackmail scheme."

"He didn't go through with it. You can't punish him just for thinking something."

"Wyatt's not completely innocent in all this, Billie. He withheld information. Obstructed the investigation. Things might have gone a lot differently if he'd—"

"He was scared! He's just a kid. Older than me but not really. And what good would saying something have done?" She sank back into the seat. "Adam Leary is a pig. You've got to hit him where it hurts. He's got lawyers he pays lots of money to just so he doesn't have to worry about going to jail."

I looked over at her, struck by the comment, another piece falling into place.

. . .

Billie didn't say anything as we walked into the house. Charley was in bed, resting. Wyatt and Kathy were sitting outside on the deck steps, having what looked like an intense conversation. Billie stepped up to the closed sliding doors and watched them, though she was unable to hear what they were saying.

"You can go out," I said. "It's okay."

"Could I get a glass of water first?" I sensed a hint of jealousy from her. Maybe it bothered her seeing Wyatt so engaged talking to someone his own age.

"Sure," I said. "Come on." I put a hand on her shoulder and guided her to the kitchen. "Glasses are up there," I said, pointing to the cupboard over the sink. "I'll be right back." I left her alone and went to talk with Charley.

She was in bed, reading a book on burn trauma.

"Talk about a crowded house," I said. She closed the tome and set it aside as I sat on the edge of the bed. "Billie said something in the car I can't shake. Why would a powerful man like Adam Leary, one with a penthouse of lawyers at his disposal, and facing a slew of sexual harassment charges, drive to a teenager's house in his son's car and brutally murder a sixteen-year-old girl?"

She frowned. "Because he's a psychopath?"

"I don't read him that way. He's a fighter. Murder, like suicide, is a coward's way out. Leary's tougher than that."

"Tough doesn't make him strong. If it's true he drugs teenage girls to sleep with them, he's the lowest despicable coward I can imagine." I nodded but said nothing. "He shot a man in his study, right? Point blank. The one he wanted you to think was him."

"I bet he didn't pull the trigger," I said. "Some lackey took care of it. Some Hollywood fixer he paid. That's more his style."

"If he didn't kill Janis, who do you think did?"

I told her about the photos sent to Janis, of her in bed with Adam, and the words that had been written across them: *Slut. Pig. Bitch. Corpse.* "Whoever sent those to her killed her."

"Wyatt?"

"I don't think so. To what end?"

"That leaves Paige in this playbook," Charley said. "But, again, why? She was a victim of Paige's father. Adam forced himself on her."

"Transference, maybe," I said. "Paige took his rage at his father out on Janis. Then he got scared Billie saw something or knew something. When Anna fled town with her, he tracked them, following Wyatt. He killed Catherine Zeigler because she got in the way. He tried to kill Anna, assuming whatever Billie knew, she'd told her mom. Billie only escaped death because she hid out in that old car."

"I could buy that," Charley said. "At least it's somewhere to start. What about Caruso?"

"I'm about to call him."

She picked up a damp towel from the bedside table and gently patted it against her burned cheek and neck. "Those poor kids."

"The world we live in," I said.

"*Part* of the world we live in," Charley said. "The other part has people in it like you."

"And you."

She shook her head and attempted a laugh. "I'm damaged goods."

"Who isn't? It just makes you more human. And you're still the most beautiful woman I know. Inside and out." I leaned in and kissed her forehead, then her burned cheek, then her lips.

. . .

"It could work," Caruso told me. I'd run my theory by him, as well as a new plan. "You set it in motion. But then we take over. Clear?"

"I'm fine with that," I said. "But I want to be there."

"Let me know once we're a go."

Billie and Wyatt were in the living room with Kathy and Charley. Kathy had given Billie a change of clothes. The shirtsleeves and pants legs were too long for her smaller and shorter frame, but the young girl didn't seem to care. I think she was just grateful to be out of the clothes she'd worn for three days straight.

I told Wyatt and Billie what I wanted to do.

"He's not going to go for it," Wyatt said.

"Maybe not. But we won't know until we try. Hand me your phone." Wyatt reluctantly took out his cell and passed it to me. "What's the passcode?"

"PSYCHO," he said.

I punched in the corresponding numbers: 779246. When his screen opened to the home page, I tapped the phone icon, then searched his contacts for Paige's phone number. "Will this connect to his new device? He deactivated one recently."

"That's the most recent."

I dialed the number, just to be sure Wyatt spoke with his brother and not someone else, trying to fool me—then handed him the phone. When the call connected, he put it on speaker so we could hear both sides of the conversation.

"Paige, it's me," Wyatt said. "Where are you? What happened to Dad?"

"Jesus, Wyatt," Paige said, his voice distant and tinny through the small speaker, but still sounding juiced up, either from adrenaline or something pharmaceutical. "Where have *you* been?"

"Is he really dead?" I'd told Wyatt before calling that it was imperative he not give Paige any indication he knew the truth about their father.

"How did you find out?"

"Some detective came by to talk to me," Wyatt said. "Guy named Caruso. Why would he do it, Paige? Why would he kill himself?"

"Guilt, bro, why do you think? He couldn't live with all the shit he'd done."

"You talking about Billie's sister?"

"I'm talking about everything," Paige said. "Where are you now? We should meet up. We're all we've got left."

"I'm at Daphne and Mia's, but I'm going home. I need to see where it happened."

"No dude, bad idea. Stay away from the house. It's a mess. You won't be able to handle it."

"You've been there?"

"Yeah, it's fucked up," Paige said. "Where's Billie? Are the police still holding her?"

Wyatt looked at me. We'd come to the question I'd expected Paige to ask. The part of the plan Wyatt didn't like, but the pin on which everything else hinged. "No, they released her."

"What does she think happened?"

Wyatt glanced at Billie and said, "She still doesn't remember everything. But some stuff from that night is coming back to her."

"Like what?"

"She won't tell me. She doesn't like talking about it. She's meeting me at the house. I'm going to pack some things, then we're both taking off. We're leaving LA tonight." Paige was silent for a good long bit. "Paige, you still there?"

"Yeah, I'm here. It's a good idea. Leaving town. Do you need anything?"

"Money. I know Dad kept cash in his safe. But I don't know how to get into it."

"I do," Paige said. "I'll meet you there."

"You sure?" Wyatt said.

"Yeah. Of course. I want to help. Wait for me if you get there first."

"Okay. And Paige? Thanks." Wyatt ended the call.

"Good job," I said.

"I just sold the guy out," Wyatt said.

"You mean the one who probably killed my sister?" Billie said.

"We don't know that. I still think my father killed her. Look at what he's done. It all points to him being guilty."

"Except the rage," I said. "Adam didn't care about Janis. She was a nuisance to him. Whoever killed her the way she was butchered cared too much."

Billie turned away, closing her eyes. I looked at my watch. Caruso and his team would be at the Leary house in fifteen minutes. I'd have to hurry to make it over the hill in time to join them.

29

I parked three blocks from the home and walked the rest of the way, passing a few locals out taking evening strolls and walking their dogs. Some gave me a nod, others said a brief, "Good evening." Most were so caught up in their own thoughts, I doubted they even noticed my presence. I spotted Caruso's sedan first, half a block down, his thin frame a meek silhouette behind the wheel. The red glow of a cigarette tip occasionally lit up when he took a drag. Apparently, the death sentence of his lung cancer had given him a reason to start smoking again. Or this case had. A taller man sat beside him. His partner, Gerald Briggs, I assumed: the man who hated my guts.

They'd picked a prime spot on the block, far enough away from any streetlamp spill, but close enough to see the Learys' front lawn. The plan was to let Paige arrive and go in, then follow, nab him, and take him in for questioning. There was, of course, the risk he wouldn't show. Or he'd figure out Wyatt and Billie weren't inside and take off before we could get to him.

I looked over at the house. The driveway was empty, the

interior of the building dark. Then a splatter of light bounced off a second-floor side window and danced across the ceiling of the room. It seemed Paige had beaten us here. Maybe he had already been in the house when Wyatt phoned. From the angle of his parked car, Caruso would not have seen the flashlight movement, so I took out my phone, set it to silent, then sent a quick text: *Someone in house. Upstairs.* Caruso shot back: *Got it. Stand down.*

I looked toward his car, saw him open his door and get out. He had his phone in his hand and was saying something into it. A moment later, a black and white cruiser eased around a corner, its headlights off. I crept forward, staying in the shadows on the opposite side of the street, watching Caruso and Briggs advance toward the house. The police cruiser moved alongside them, keeping their pace. I crossed the street.

"Far side of the house," I said, pointing as I joined them. "Flashlight beam in the window. Second floor. Could be Paige, could be Adam. All I saw was the light."

Caruso said to me, "Stay here," then he and Briggs headed for the front door, Briggs ignoring me completely. The cruiser pulled into the driveway. Two officers got out. They followed the detectives across the grass to the front porch.

Caruso knocked on the door, waited, then knocked again. Not surprisingly, no one answered. He motioned to one of the two officers. The officer kicked at the front door with his right foot. The door swung inward. The other officer entered first, gun drawn, followed by his partner, then Briggs, and finally Caruso.

As I waited and watched and fidgeted, movement down the street caught my eye. Someone on foot had come around the same corner as the patrol car. He walked briskly, hands in his pockets, black cap pulled down on his brow. If it weren't for his height, I'd have assumed he was simply another local out for a stroll. But the odds of another man *that* tall, coming down *this* street, moving toward *this* house, were a million to one.

It was him, no question.

Adam Leary kept his gaze down as he approached—probably worried a neighbor might spot and recognize him. I moved to the far side of a wide tree between the sidewalk and the street. Leary didn't see the patrol car parked in his driveway until he'd almost reached his yard. At that point, it was easy for me to come out of hiding, grab him, and push him face down on the trunk hood.

"What the hell?" he said. "Let me go. I live here."

I turned him over so he could see my face and said, "I know that." I grabbed his jacket and pulled him up straight, removing the Beretta from my waistband with my free hand and pushing the barrel tip against his chest.

"Chance? What are you doing here?"

I ignored the question and asked my own. "Is Paige inside?"

"How the hell should I know?"

"Dead men know nothing?"

"What in God's name is that supposed to mean?" His exaggerated confusion was almost comical.

"Spare me the histrionics," I said. "Leave that to your attorney." I pushed him away but kept the gun trained on him, then took my cell phone out, and called Caruso.

"Adam's outside with me," I said. "He's immobilized. Is Paige in there?"

"No sign of him," Caruso said. "Just the woman, Angelique Tourneau. She was cleaning out the safe."

"I need an officer out here," I told Caruso.

"One's on the way."

I dragged Adam across the lawn to the front door, where I was met by one of the uniformed officers. Caruso, Briggs, and the other officer exited soon after with Angelique Tourneau in handcuffs.

"You have no idea the world of shit you just stepped in," Leary said, as the first officer cuffed him, led him to the patrol cruiser, and forced him into the backseat. Before the door slammed shut, Leary demanded to know what I was staring at.

I told him I was looking for a trace of humanity.

"I willingly admit I'm morally bankrupt," he said. "I don't pretend otherwise. It's a Godless town, Chance. I sleep fine at night."

"I'll give Anna Ryker your condolences," I said, as the second cop placed Angelique in the backseat beside Adam.

"Where's your son Paige?" Caruso asked.

"I have no idea," Leary said, and turned away.

The first officer shut the door. He and the second officer got in the front seat. The cruiser backed out onto the street and drove off.

"Fat chance Paige shows up now," Briggs said, glaring at me as if I'd blundered something. "The guy probably witnessed the whole thing and took off."

"Let's give it another half hour," Caruso said.

We went to Caruso's car and got in to wait. I sat in the back, Briggs and Caruso in the front. I said to Briggs, "We haven't officially met. I'm Jason Chance."

"I know who you are," Briggs said, keeping his gaze forward, through the windshield.

"Don't be a prick, Gerry. We should be thanking him. He's a hell of a cop."

Briggs had nothing to say to that.

Caruso lit another cigarette. "No point in denying myself the pleasure now."

"I'm sorry you're facing this," I told him.

"You and me both."

We waited for thirty minutes, most of it in silence. Caruso smoked and Briggs kept looking at his phone. I stared over at the dark and empty Leary house.

Paige never showed.

WALKING BACK TO MY CAR, I CALLED CHARLEY'S CELL PHONE. She didn't pick up. Neither did Kathy on hers. No one answered my house line. I'd input Billie's and Wyatt's numbers into my phone, and when I called them, neither responded.

Something was wrong.

I raced through three red lights as I headed home. When I turned on my street, I saw a fire truck and ambulance parked at a house mid-block. Two uniformed LAPD officers, a couple of paramedics, and a fireman were on the lawn of the home, talking to a man in pajamas. I drove past, on to my house. The LAPD cruiser Caruso had placed outside as security sat empty at the curb. I left my car door open and ran to the front door. I fumbled to get the right key, jammed it in the lock, turned it, and swung open the door. Stepping into the house, I raised my gun.

"Kathy?" I shouted. No response came. "Charley!"

More silence.

I went into my daughter's room first. She lay on her side, uncovered and in PJs, her eyes closed. Her chest rose and fell steadily with each breath. Relieved, I crossed the alcove and entered our bedroom. Charley was on her back, also uncovered, wearing her compression top. She, too, breathed normally.

"Charley? Charley, wake up." I gently shook her unburned shoulder. She didn't respond. "Charley, come on." She moaned but remained unconscious. I looked over at the nightstand, at her creams and bottles of pills, and at an empty tea mug.

Returning to Kathy's room, I saw a similar mug on the bedside table, half-drunk.

"Billie?" I called out. "Wyatt?"

I checked the bathroom then looked in my study. Both rooms were empty. I headed down the hallway toward the back of the house. The living room was in disarray: lamps overturned and shattered, a bookcase toppled to the floor. The patio door was open.

I stepped out onto the back deck and down onto the grass. My movement triggered the security light. In its brightness, I saw a figure on the ground near the retaining wall, tangled in the downed bougainvillea and trellis pieces. I hurried over. Paige Leary lay face up, his chest and abdomen covered in blood. His eyes darted left and right, frantically. His breath was low and wheezing. A kitchen knife lay on the grass near his left hand.

I took out my phone to call for help. Paige reached up and grabbed my arm, shaking his head.

"Waste ... of ... time," he said, his voice garbled and wet. "Dying fast ..."

He was right about that.

30

"Anything you want to say before it's over, Paige?" I discreetly turned on the recording app on my phone.

"She ... broke ... my ... heart."

"Who did? Janis? Did you kill her?"

"Didn't deserve ... to live ... Not after ..."

"Your father raped her, Paige. It wasn't her fault."

"It's always ... their fault."

With that last, despicable statement—a summation of the way this man, and his father, looked at women—life faded from his eyes.

I returned to the house. I doubted I'd find Wyatt or Billie. The scenario had already started to come together in my head. I called Caruso.

"Paige Leary's dead," I told him. "Wyatt and Billie are missing. They may have killed him. He pretty much confessed to me to killing Janis."

"Son of bitch," he muttered, barely above a whisper. "Stay there. I mean it. Don't go anywhere. I'm on my way with a team."

. . .

THE EMERGENCY MEDICAL TEAM FROM THE INCIDENT DOWN the street responded to the call, as there had been no injuries at the other site—confirming for me that the incident (a fire in the backyard) was staged for distraction, most likely by Paige. There was nothing the paramedics could do to save him; he was dead by the time they arrived. They stabilized Charley and Kathy with oxygen masks and checked their vital signs. Both were groggy and disoriented, had no idea what happened. The last thing each remembered was getting in bed and falling asleep.

"How long ago?" I asked.

"About an hour," Charley said.

"Who made the tea before you went to bed?"

"Billie and Wyatt," Kathy said.

I had no doubt a toxicology report would find a sedative of some kind in their system and residue of it in the tea mugs; Billie and/or Wyatt had probably taken a few of Charley's morphine pills and used them to knock the two out.

Why had Paige come to my house? Was he on to our plan from the beginning? Or had Wyatt gotten back in touch with him after I left, to tell him about the trap he'd be walking into at their father's house? Luring him here instead.

Caruso eventually arrived with two officers and a team from the ME's office. They examined Paige's body and carted it away.

"Still think they're just babes in the woods?" Caruso asked me, referring to Billie and Wyatt.

"More like damaged souls," I said.

"Where would they go?"

"I'm guessing back to the desert. To Anna. They're going to run, for sure. But I'll bet my life Billie's going to say goodbye to her mom first."

I wanted Kathy and Charley to go to the hospital to be checked out. Both refused. Charley said she did a count of the morphine pills left in her bottle. Since her accidental overdose, she'd been diligent in keeping track. Four pills were missing. Which meant Kathy and she had each been given two 30 mg tablet doses.

"The paramedics have already given us naloxone," Charley said. "Which is what they would do if we'd gone to the ER. 60 mg isn't going to do lasting damage to Kathy. And I didn't take my dosage this evening because I wanted to stay alert and sleep lightly in case I needed to get up. I'm used to taking 30 mg at a time. Doubling that once isn't going to kill me."

"I'm not leaving you both here alone," I said.

"Then I guess we're all taking a road trip," Kathy said.

CARUSO CONTACTED DETECTIVE ROONEY IN INDIO AND TOLD him to be on the lookout for Billie Ryker and Wyatt Leary, that they'd possibly be coming to see Anna Ryker. She was still in the hospital, and under police guard. He sent a DMV photo of Wyatt and the arrest photo for Billie. "Both teenagers should be taken into custody on sight," he said.

"I'm going with you to Indio to pick up the kids," I told Caruso.

"You really are a glutton for punishment," he said.

"I started this. I need to see it through to the end."

"I hope you see the irony here. At the end of the day, we're still going to bring her in for murder."

"We don't know who did the stabbing," I said.

"She had the most motive. This was a revenge killing. Paige was stabbed the way Janis had been. Papa Leary's lucky he's locked up, or Billie might have gone to work on him, too."

"What is it about her, Dante? She'll never be innocent in your eyes, will she?"

"No," Caruso said. "And I wish I could explain why. But I can't."

I almost felt pity for his dilemma.

"Did you ever get an ID on the body you first thought was Adam Leary's?" I asked, just to change the subject.

Caruso shook his head. "One more thing we're going to have to pry out of the guy. So far, he's not talking and has lawyered up, as has the Tourneau woman."

"Perhaps the news of his son's murder will break him."

"Don't hold your breath. You think there's even a shred of a conscience there? He said it himself. He's morally bankrupt."

Indeed he was. Rotten to the core of his Hollywood soul. He'd passed this along to Paige, for sure, but I wanted to believe Wyatt was still capable of saving.

CARUSO RODE IN THE PATROL CAR WITH THE TWO DEPUTIES. I followed in my car with Kathy and Charley. It was an easy drive at that time of night. We arrived at the hospital in Indio to news from Detective Rooney that there'd been no sign of either Billie Ryker or Wyatt Leary.

The medical center was dark and practically empty. As we rode up in the elevator to the second floor, I asked Caruso to give me five minutes alone with Anna. "She'll be more candid with me," I said. "If she's had any contact with Billie, I believe I can get her to admit it."

"Hey, if you can, more power to you," he said, looking more tired than I'd ever seen him. "I doubt she'll tell *me* squat. I'm public enemy number one in her world."

"Do you blame her?"

"I wish she knew it was never personal. I've hated every second of this case."

I could think of nothing to say to contradict that or make him feel better.

As we approached Anna's door, I said to Kathy and Charley, "Come in with me. Both of you," then pushed open the room door and let them enter first. Anna was propped up in bed. Her eyes widened with anticipation when she saw me.

"Where's Billie?"

"You haven't heard from her?"

"No." The anticipation turned to fear.

"Are you sure?"

"Oh God," she whispered. "What's happened now?"

"I suspect she's on her way here," I said. "There's a lot to tell you."

Anna looked from me to Kathy to Charley. Charley approached the bed. Anna reached out and took her hand. "You must be Charlotte."

"Call me Charley. And I'm so sorry about all that's happened to you. Especially the loss of Janis."

"Thank you." She glanced over at my daughter. "Hello, Kathy."

"Doctor Ryker, I wanted to call you after I learned, but then everything went ..."

"Crazy," Anna finished the phrase, nodding her head. "I know. It certainly did. How are you doing? How are you feeling?"

"Good. Better. That doesn't matter, though. Not right now."

"Of course, it matters. And I'm very happy to hear it." Anna then went silent, looking at me.

"Paige Leary is dead," I told her. "He confessed to me that he killed Janis. I believe it was a jealousy killing, over details I will tell you another time. Wyatt and Billie are together and on the run. I think she'll come to see you before they do anything else. I thought she would have been here already. Or at least called you."

Anna struggled to sit forward. "You said she was in custody. You told me she'd be safer there."

"Once evidence against Paige emerged, the police had no choice but to release her."

"Why is she on the run? I don't understand."

"Wyatt and Billie lured Paige to my house," I said. "They drugged Kathy and Charley. When I got there, they were gone. I found Paige in the backyard. He'd been stabbed, many times, with a knife from our kitchen. He lived only long enough to confess to killing Janis."

"Oh dear lord," Anna whispered. "This is all out of control."

She reached for the IV in her arm. The simple movement caused her great pain but didn't stop her.

"Anna, don't," I said.

Charley rested a hand on her shoulder. Anna shrugged it off and swung her legs over the edge of the bed. She dropped to her feet. The sudden movement made her lightheaded. She tottered forward, threatening to fall. Charley grabbed her and steadied her. I took her other arm.

"Billie didn't kill Paige," Anna said. "There's no way. It's all on the brother. Wyatt. He had to have acted alone. Billie's confused, she's ... lost."

"That's why she needs our help," I said. "We have to convince her and Wyatt to turn themselves in."

The landline phone beside the bed rang with a shrill blast.

"Answer it," I said.

Anna sat back on the bed and picked up the receiver. "Hello?" She paused, listening to whoever was on the other end. She gripped the receiver with both hands. "Billie, where are you?"

31

Winds like the night before had returned. The parking lot was blanketed in swirling dirt and sand. It had come on quick and heavy, as is often the case with desert storms, and my Wrangler was coated with half an inch of dust. I got behind the wheel, turned on the wipers to clear the windshield, and headed out of the lot.

It took fifteen minutes to reach the Zeigler home. A patrol car's flashing lights cut through the opaque air as I turned onto Gaviota. The cruiser's doors were open and Steen and Zeravsky had taken shooter's stances behind them.

I stopped in the middle of the street and got out of the Jeep. Steen shouted, "Sir, get back in your car. Reverse and drive away."

"It's me, Jason Chance," I answered, calling out over the moaning wind. "What's going on?"

"Shots fired. Second floor window."

"Have you had any communications with them?"

"Negative," Zeravsky said. "We've contacted Indio PD. Negotiators and a SWAT team are on the way."

A SWAT team. The last thing I wanted to hear. This could go bad in so many ways.

"I know the two people inside," I said. "They're scared teenagers. I can talk to them."

"We have orders to wait for the negotiators, Mister Chance," Zeravsky said.

"They won't be able to end this," I said. "They'll probably make things worse." I started toward the front lawn, looking up at the window from which the shots had been fired.

"Mister Chance, get back to your vehicle!"

"You want to stop me, shoot me." I stepped onto the sidewalk and yelled toward the house, "Billie? Wyatt? It's me, Jason." I took my Beretta from my waist and set it on the ground. "I'm unarmed, and I'm coming in." I kept moving toward the front door. The officers didn't do anything to stop me, and no shots were fired from inside. I reached the entrance, turned the unlocked knob, pushed open the door, and entered the dark foyer.

Billie stood at the top of the curving staircase, looking down.

"How'd they know we were here?" she asked.

"They had a trace on your mom's hospital room phone."

"Fuck," she whispered. "I called from here so they wouldn't know it was me."

"We're never as smart as we think we are."

"I'm learning that," she said.

"Who shot at the cops?"

"Wyatt. He's got a shotgun. It was in his car. I didn't even know. He just wanted to scare them off, so they wouldn't try to come inside."

"What happened back at my place, Billie? With Paige?"

"You should come on up," she said, then turned and headed along the second-floor corridor.

I bounded up the stairs and followed her into the first bedroom. Wyatt stood near the window holding a Winchester 12-gauge that seemed oversized in his small hands and against his scrawny frame. He'd changed clothes since my house, and his hair was wet.

"Put the gun down, Wyatt," I said. "If you shoot a cop, your problems will go from bad to unbeatable."

"That's what I've been telling him," Billie said.

"If you're so worried, just let us go," Wyatt said to me. "We don't want to hurt anybody. We just want to run away. Disappear."

"There's no disappearing now, Wyatt. Not after what happened to Paige."

"Paige? Didn't you catch him? Wasn't that your plan? The one I sold him out for."

"I've been to my house. I've seen his body. There may still be a way out of this for you, but you've got to tell me what happened."

"We put morphine in their tea so they'd sleep," Billie said. "And we ran. We took your daughter's car. That's it. That's everything."

"Stop it," I said.

Wyatt looked at Billie. She said, "We didn't kill him, Mister Chance. He wasn't even there when we left." Her voice was calm and steady, her eyes never straying from Wyatt. "Right?"

He nodded, barely. They'd clearly rehearsed this.

"He wasn't quite dead when I got to him," I said. "He told me a lot of things." I had no problem letting them think Paige ratted them out if it got them to tell the truth. "There are a lot of ways a good attorney could spin it. He came there to kill you. It was self-defense. You had no choice. But you can't keep lying about it. You've got to tell me everything. Let me help you through this. No more running. Put the gun down and turn yourselves in."

"I do that, my life's over," Wyatt said.

"No," I said. "It's over if you try to run."

Wyatt started pacing back and forth.

"Get away from the window," Billie shouted.

"Just give me the gun," I said. "We can put this right. There's still time."

"No," Wyatt said. "I don't trust you. I don't trust anybody anymore." He glanced at Billie. "Except you. Only you." He paused. "I'll do what you want."

Billie leaned back, knocking her head against the wall, gently and repeatedly, as if trying to shake loose the right answer. Outside, a siren wailed—another cruiser arriving. Police lights sliced through the thick sand of the windstorm, reminiscent of a light show during a rock concert. Only there was no music to accompany this display. No exuberance. No joy.

More cops would come as this dragged out. The passage of time during standoffs increases the level of perceived danger. Everybody gets tense. One false move and it all goes to hell.

"The army's here, guys," I said. "They're going to escort you out, one way or another." I took a step toward Billie. "You've got to make a choice."

Anna's voice on a loudspeaker rose above the howl of the wind. "Billie? Billie, baby, are you okay? It's Mom."

Hearing her voice, Billie burst into tears. She shouted, "I can't take it. I don't want to be a part of this any longer. I don't want to act this way anymore."

"Then do the right thing," I said.

She regarded me with such uncertainty and fear, my heart swelled. She was the little black-haired girl in her favorite song by the Cure, "One Hundred Years," *waiting for Saturday*. Her father's death *pushing her, pushing her.* Losing him had forced her to grow up way too fast and, at the same time, kept her forever a child.

Wyatt saw it, too. I think it scared him. He held the rifle out, holding it horizontally with both hands, so I could take it from him. Once I had, he stepped over to Billie and wrapped his arms around her and let her cry into his shirt. I saw the depth of his love for her then, and I knew every action he'd made had been because of it.

32

We walked in a single file down the stairs. Billie led the way. Wyatt followed. I brought up the rear. When we'd reached the foyer, I said, "Hold on," and stepped in front of them. I gently pushed them out of the line of fire and opened the front door. Stepping out onto the porch, I held up the rifle. "We're coming out," I shouted.

Detective Rooney yelled, "Hold your fire!"

There were three squad cars positioned in zigzagged formation on the street in front of the house. The red and blue flashing lights on the roofs of the vehicles cut through the density of the storm. Sand crystals danced in their glow. The officers were stationed on the far sides of the cars, their guns resting on the hoods. Anna stood beside Detective Caruso and Detective Rooney. Charley and Kathy were behind her.

When she spotted Billie, Anna broke away from the group, dodging between the police cars and rushing up the walkway toward us, ignoring Caruso's calls for her to stop.

Billie ran to meet her halfway. Mother and daughter came together in a fierce embrace.

Caruso arrested Billie and Wyatt because he had no choice. He took Anna Ryker into custody for aiding and abetting a felon. She would be kept under guard overnight in Kennedy Hospital. Billie and Wyatt would spend the night in the local jail. Under interrogation by Caruso and myself, Wyatt confessed to killing his brother.

"The more I thought about what you said, Mister Chance, the more sense it made," Wyatt admitted. "My father wouldn't have killed Janis. It wasn't his style. He's the kind of man who needs to hide behind money for everything. He'd take his chances in court. Or he'd run, like he tried to do. But Paige had no boundaries and thought of himself as invincible. Remember the girl he used in that short film he made? She had a nervous breakdown after they shot it. You know why? Paige pushed her over the edge. Did sick things to her to scare her and get a more honest performance. Secretly stalked her while she was alone at home, making late-night phone calls to her. He even hired some other student to follow her around, in parking lots and shit. He snuck into her apartment and left scary things there, like dead animals and blood on her bed sheets. She called the cops on him but they could never prove he had anything to do with it. Or maybe Dad took care of it for him. Paige said he thought it was cool because he'd read it's what Hitchcock did to his leading ladies. But know what I really think? He got a kick out of bullying and torturing women. The movie just gave him an excuse to do it."

"Why did Paige go to my house tonight?" I asked him.

"Because I called him as soon as you left and told him to

forget about the money, that Billie and I had changed our minds, and we weren't leaving town. Then I said I knew he killed Janis. And I was disgusted. That I was going to go to the cops."

"You figured he'd come get you," Caruso said.

"Yeah. So I made tea for Kathy and Miss Frasier with some of that morphine she takes. I'd noticed the pill bottle earlier, in your bedroom, when I went in to ask Miss Frasier if she wanted something to eat. Later, when she went to the bathroom, I took four and put two each in their mugs."

"Billie knew what you were doing all along?" Caruso asked.

"No. I didn't want her knowing what I was up to until after I'd done it."

"You mean kill him," Caruso said.

"Yeah." Wyatt leaned back in his chair, the reality of his actions catching up with him. "I just wanted to keep Billie safe. I figured the only way for that was if Paige was dead. He wasn't going to jail. There was no evidence. Plus, he deserved it for what he did to Janis."

"Like you say, there was no evidence," Caruso said. "You had no proof he killed her."

"He confessed it to me. At your house."

"That's not proof. That's just something you're saying."

"Sometimes the only proof you have is knowing it's true."

I mulled that over. "What happened when he showed up?"

"I'd left the back door unlocked, then Billie and I hid in the garage. The plan was, we'd knock him out when he came searching for us, then take him somewhere else in Kathy's car. The keys were there on that alcove desk. I didn't want to kill him in your home." He paused, staring at his balled-up hands. "Things didn't go as planned."

"How so?" I asked.

"Paige was harder to subdue than I thought he'd be. Stronger. He fought back. When I thought I had him down, I told Billie to go get some rope I'd seen in the kitchen. She ran out. Paige was able to push me off and chase after her. She kept running through the house, throwing shit at him, finally running outside, into the backyard." This explained the mess of broken items in my living room. "I grabbed a knife from a kitchen drawer. When I came outside, Paige was on top of her. He was choking her. I went crazy, pushing him off and sitting on him, pinning him down. Then I just started stabbing. In his chest, his neck, his arms. At one point I could hardly see because there was blood in my eyes. His blood. Billie finally had to stop me. I threw the knife down beside his body. Billie said, 'We've got to get out of here.' I was in a daze. I just kept staring down at Paige. He wasn't even my brother anymore. He was some dangerous animal I'd killed."

The air in the interrogation room had grown cold and thick. My lungs felt heavy. I'd listened to murder confessions before, but this one was difficult to take in. I had to remind myself it came from a seventeen-year-old boy. "You thought he was dead."

"Yeah."

"Billie said, 'Come on, Wyatt. We have to leave.' She grabbed my arm and pulled me to my feet. I didn't fight back or argue. She took me outside and told me I had to pull myself together so I could drive, because she didn't know how. We took off in Kathy's car. I didn't even know where we were going. Billie guided me. I drove on autopilot all the way here, to the desert. The Zeigler house was unlocked. I took a shower in the room Billie had been using and washed all his blood off. Billie gave me a pair of her jeans and a T-shirt." He looked down at his clothes. "These are hers." He paused. "Then the cops came, and you know the rest."

"Yes, we do," Caruso said.

Wyatt looked almost relieved. The catharsis of release.

"Billie's going to be all right now, isn't she?" he asked. "She's off the hook. She didn't kill Janis. And it wasn't her fault her mother dragged her out to the desert. She's innocent."

I looked at Caruso. Caruso shrugged. "We'll have to see."

Something occurred to me then. "How'd you get the gun you used in the desert?" I asked. "Billie said you'd been carrying it around in your car for a couple of days. But your car is at Daphne and Mia's. You took Kathy's car to the desert."

"Billie was confused. I found the gun in Mrs. Zeigler's house."

"No, you didn't, Wyatt. Catherine Zeigler didn't own guns. And the police searched your car after Billie told us she'd spotted it near her house the night of Janis's murder. There was no gun there, either." I paused. "Those aren't Billie's clothes, they're yours. You went home after you left my place. You and Billie. And you got the gun from the house. You went there for it, and to get the money out of the safe, right? Why lie about that when you've confessed to everything else?"

He looked up at me with an expression that seemed to say, *'Go on, figure it out.'*

"That shotgun was the one used to kill the man in your father's study," I said. "The man he wanted us to believe was him."

Wyatt nodded.

"You still thought you could blackmail him," I said.

"He's going to beat any charges you try to pin on him. I wanted to make him pay where it hurts. He owes me. And he owes Billie."

"Who's the man that got shot?"

"Martin. The guy that cleans our pool."

"How do you know that?"

"I recognized a scar on his arm when I looked at those photos at the morgue."

"You didn't think to say something?" Caruso said.

"Why tell us anything?" I said, then looked at Wyatt. "You'd already figured out this new way to get at your dad, hadn't you?"

Wyatt shrugged. "It's a cold, cruel world," he said. "You do what you've got to do."

Right there, in front of my eyes, I watched the last vestige of his adolescence die.

CHARLEY AND KATHY HAD TAKEN KATHY'S CAR BACK TO LA before Caruso and I interrogated Wyatt. I wanted to go home, too, but I needed to make one final stop. The night seemed darker than normal around me as I drove away from the Indio police station, as if a black tarp had been thrown over the desert. The temperature felt colder than when I'd arrived, and I couldn't escape the scent of blood in the air.

"CARUSO SAYS THE DA IS DROPPING ALL CHARGES AGAINST Billie and you," I told Anna, back in her hospital room. "They'll release Billie in the morning. Once you're strong enough, you both can go home."

"What about Wyatt?"

"Things don't look as optimistic, I'm afraid. If he gets a good lawyer, he might come out okay."

"That poor boy."

"It's tricky. Self-defense will be a tough sell. The prosecution will argue premeditation, that his intention was to lure Paige to my house. It'll come down to how the defense can spin Paige's attack on Billie."

"Is any of this going to blow back on her?"

"Probably not. I'll do whatever I can to make sure. So will Wyatt. As crazy as it all is, there's one thing I'm sure of. He loves Billie. He'll do anything to protect her."

Anna shook her head. "It can never be. The two of them. If I had known, I would have stopped it."

"I doubt you could have," I said, and gave her a sad smile. "They do what they do. Most of the time, we can only watch and pray we've given them the skills to do right."

"Obviously, I failed."

"No. Billie is guilty of nothing in all this. That's your proof."

It was close to 4 a.m. when I got back home. Kathy was asleep in bed. Charley had dozed off on the living room couch, a book butterflied on her chest. The women had cleaned up as much of the mess from the earlier violence as they could, but signs of the CSU's forensic investigation were still in evidence: black fingerprint dust on the handle of the patio door, yellow numbered evidence markers left behind outside, where Paige had gone down. I shut off the backyard light, blacking out the reminder.

I turned and looked down at Charley, my heart swelling with love for this woman I'd almost lost from my life only a few months ago. There are not many things more damaging to the human spirit than loss. Too often, we spend our time living in fear of losing what we most love, when instead we should be embracing the fact that we haven't lost it yet.

The horrors of being human cripple us.

Charley stirred and opened her eyes.

"You okay?" she asked.

"I am now," I said, and sat beside her.

"What happened?"

"Wyatt confessed to killing his brother. Billie and Anna have been exonerated of all charges. It's over."

Kathy, who must have been awakened by my arrival, joined us.

"I had another dream," she said, her eyes still cloudy from sleep. "I think this might be the last one. Like Janis knows she can move on." She sat on the floor before us, her legs crossed. "I was back in her room, but it was different somehow. Clean, cheerful, like it was before. She looked younger, her skin rosy, her eyes filled with life. She seemed happy, too. She had a photo in her hand, of Billie and her mom, with her. They were on a beach, arms around each other, while Janis held her phone up to take the selfie. It was just simple and ordinary and ... nice."

"A beautiful image to end with," Charley said.

I agreed. I don't doubt there are ghosts among us. And angels. It's a mysterious world.

33

Charley and I married six weeks later, under the stars on a beach in Malibu, with twenty of our closest friends attending. Anna and Billie were there. Wyatt was not. He'd gotten a good lawyer, though, who pled the charges down from second-degree murder to manslaughter, due to provocation and heat of passion, and by pleading guilty at the arraignment, he was sentenced to only three years. He'd possibly be out in eighteen months.

I'd invited Dante Caruso to the wedding but received news three days before the ceremony that he'd finally succumbed to the cancer that gripped him. He died alone in his sleep, found the next morning by a housekeeper. The news made me sad.

Marty and Lenny came, and some of Kathy's friends from school. Charley's mother and sister drove down from Oakland. Harry Feiffer and several other officers and detectives—friends and colleagues from my time at the sheriff's department—attended, too. I wanted to believe Captain Ellison was watching from above and smiling. It was a happy, united gathering. We stayed on the beach after and had a small celebration with a bonfire, catered BBQ from Barrel and Ash, an 80s new wave cover band, and booze courtesy of Lenny and Marty.

A good time was had by all, as they say.

Charley looked beautiful, a radiant angel in white. Bare shouldered, she refused to hide her burn scars. "Life is all or nothing," she said. "I'm learning to embrace that philosophy."

"Good," I said. "Maybe you can teach me, as well."

At one point, late in the evening, as the guest count dwindled down, I spotted Billie sitting alone on the sand, close to the shoreline. I walked down to her.

"Feel like some company?" I asked. She nodded, so I sat. "How are you doing?"

"Better," she said. "I've been dreaming about her lately. Janis. In a good way. I see her in a happy place. You set her free."

"I don't think I can take credit for that."

"Just accept the compliment, okay? *Fuck*. What is it with you?" She'd grown up in the past few weeks, acquiring the jadedness of maturity. This was a wonderful and terrible thing. "Good band, by the way," she said, referring to the cover group. "I like when they play the Cure songs."

"I figured you would."

"I just wish they'd play something from this century."

"Then they wouldn't be an 80s cover band," I said. "You want me to ask them to play 'One Hundred Years'?"

"No thanks. I've kind of let that song go."

"We all move on from the things we think define us at certain times. Once they no longer do."

"Yeah. And you told me no *one thing* defines us, anyway." She looked up at me. I saw gratitude in her eyes. "I made you a wedding present." She reached into her pocket and took out a computer flash drive. "It's a couple of songs. Mom said you were like this rock and roll junkie."

I smiled. "That's a good way of putting it."

"Well, this is something I bet you never heard."

"Thank you, Billie. I'm excited to listen."

"You'll tell me what you think?"

"Of course."

"I wrote the songs, that's why I ask. These are simple versions. Just keyboards and me. Demo type."

"I had no idea you wrote music."

"Nobody did. I've kept it a secret. I taught myself how to play. I'm not very good yet."

"You'll get better. You just have to keep at it."

She smiled. "That's what Janis told me. In one of the dreams. *'Don't give up,'* she said." Billie looked off across the dark ocean. "I miss her. There's so much I wish I could go back and change. Things I want to say to her. Things I never did."

"You still can. She'll hear you."

Billie nodded. "One of the songs I wrote is about her. 'The Bad Side of Good.' I was trying to make sense of what went wrong."

"Some questions are hard to answer."

She looked at me. "Do you believe in the devil, Mr. Chance?"

"I believe there's evil in the world," I said. "I still don't understand where it comes from."

"Me either."

We sat there for a long while, both of us silent, just listening to the waves and looking at the moon glistening on the water. Eventually Charley joined us.

"You guys okay?" she asked.

"We're good," I said. "Right, Billie?"

"Yeah, we are."

Charley sat beside me. "What a beautiful night."

"And you're a beautiful bride," Billie said. Charley smiled and thanked her. "They say Wyatt may get out in a couple of years. Less, even."

"I hope that's the case," I said.

"Me too," Billie said.

"Billie, we need to get going," Anna called out, approaching. We stood up. "It was a beautiful wedding," Anna said. "I'm so happy for both of you." She leaned in and kissed Charley's undamaged cheek. Then she turned to me. "And you. God. Where to begin? I don't know how I can ever say thank you."

"You don't have to," I said.

She put her arms around me and held me close. "I'll say it anyway." And she did.

"So you'll listen to the songs?" Billie asked. "And you promise you'll tell me the truth?"

"I'll be brutally or joyously honest," I said.

"Good. And maybe you could show me some of the music you like."

"I'd love to."

Billie nodded and threw her arms around me, as well. Then Anna and she walked back toward the remains of the wedding party. I would never see Anna again, but Billie would come back into my life in a way I didn't expect.

That's a story for another day.

"You've got a new friend," Charley said.

"Seems I do."

I took my bride's hand and kissed her fingers, then her lips. A wave broke closer to us, the tide coming in. As we sat back down in the sand, I thought about how the world and beauty and love and life can sometimes be captured and crystalized in one single moment. It's easy to forget that, for every evil thing, there are a thousand good ones that come along in this crazy, dangerous, wonderful place we call home, and we must keep reminding ourselves of that fact, or we'll go mad. The horrors of being human may indeed cripple us, but the wonders of life and love build us back up. I wrapped my arm around Charley and pulled her close. She rested her head on my shoulder. Another wave splashed, and we let the cool water bathe our naked feet.

AFTERWORD

I hope you enjoyed this Jason Chance mystery. Please consider reviewing THE BAD SIDE OF GOOD on Amazon. I love reading your thoughts, and honest reviews help other readers as they make that all-important decision to read a book (or not). Long or short, whatever you feel, I'll appreciate it. Thank you so much!

Jason Chance will return in MIDNIGHT LOGIC in 2019.

ACKNOWLEDGMENTS

As always, my eternal love and thanks to:
Adriana, my first and best reader, always. This was a tough one, and you helped guide me out of the dark forest and into the light.
My daughters, Alana and Laura. Their insight into the minds of strong young women (and the mysterious teen years that shape them) was of immense help in developing the characters of Kathy, Billie, and Janis and bringing them to life.
The Los Angeles Count Sheriff's Department.
The California cities of Los Angeles and Indio.

And, as always, a HUGE thanks to you, Dear Reader, for taking this new journey with Jason, Charley, Kathy, and me.

ABOUT THE AUTHOR

Award-winning writer/producer Josh Griffith is author of the mystery novels *This Lonely Town*, *A Darkness That Blinds*, and *Torch Songs for the Dead* (books 1, 2, and 3 in the Jason Chance Series), the stand-alone novels of suspense *The Lost Man* and *The Forgotten Place*, and the action novella *Run Like Hell*. He co-authored the novel *The Killing Club* (Hyperion Books) with Michael Malone.

He is currently at work on *Just Below Sunset*, the first in a new series featuring Nick "The Nightmare" Kilborn, an offbeat private eye working the gritty streets of 1975 Los Angeles.

Jason Chance will return in 2019 in *Midnight Logic*, Book 5 in the Jason Chance series.

www.darkstreetpress.com
darkstreetpress@icloud.com

Made in the USA
Las Vegas, NV
07 October 2021